ORNAMENT OF PHARAOH

PALACE OF THE ORNAMENTS
BOOK TWO

KYLIE QUILLINAN

First published in Australia in 2023.

ABN 34 112 708 734

kyliequillinan.com

A catalogue record for this book is available from the National Library of Australia.

Ebook ISBN: 99781922852229

Paperback ISBN: 9781922852236

Large print ISBN: 9781922852489

Hardback ISBN: 9781922852243

Audiobook ISBN: 9781922852441

This is a work of fiction. Any similarity between the characters and situations within its pages and places or persons, living or dead, is unintentional and coincidental.

Cover art by 100 Covers

Edited by MS Novak.

This work uses Australian spelling and grammar.

LP16012025

For Molly.
It was never going to be long enough.

CHAPTER 1

After hours spent standing in the courtyard listening to Pharaoh's account of his own greatness and then seeing him climb into a waiting palanquin, my emotions were conflicted. On one hand, I was surprised and, if truth be told, a little offended he still hadn't called for me. But my shock at discovering Pharaoh wasn't the wise and handsome man I expected was mixed with relief at not having to face him immediately. I needed time to reconcile myself to this new image of him.

Back in my chambers, I sank onto a couch and peeled off my bangles, stacking them beside me on the cushion. They had been heavy and hot against my skin in the day's heat. And this was still *shemu*, which was supposedly not the hottest time of the year. Ahmose and Merytre stood together at a window, talking quietly as they looked out over the grounds three stories below.

"What did you think of Pharaoh?" Ettu asked as she poured herself some melon juice. She held up the jug to ask if I wanted some and I nodded. My throat was parched.

I searched for a response that would be honest enough without revealing my disgust.

"He wasn't as I expected," I said at last.

Ettu brought me a mug and I drank gratefully, as much to give myself time to think as anything else. Indeed, the flabby, pompous man we had spent half the day waiting for was nothing like I had imagined. He bore little resemblance to Khaemmalu or Sutem or any of the other Palace guards I had seen. His shaved head was where any similarity with those men ended. They had muscular physiques from working or training. He had the softness of a man who did nothing but laze around on couches and eat far too much good food.

But worse than his appearance was what I had learned about his mind. His speech, for which hundreds of Ornaments were kept standing in the sun for hours, was a monotonous accounting of his own greatness. The sun rose because of him. The Great River flooded at the appropriate time and to the most desirable height because of him. We ate and drank and were clothed because of him. Apparently everything which was right or good occurred because of Pharaoh, in his own mind at least.

He said nothing of any importance. No mention of Nebtu, who had been missing for more than a week. No discussion about politics or the state of the country or the welfare of its people. Nothing about anything other than himself.

My disappointment was my own fault really. There was no reason to expect he would be anything like I had imagined. But still, I was bitterly disillusioned. I had expected Pharaoh to be a wise and intelligent man, even if he wasn't handsome. Well educated. Someone who knew his own mind and had definite opinions, yes, but a man who took advice from those around him and considered the value of their views, like my father. Wasn't that what the ruler of a country should be like? But it was clear Pharaoh was a man who liked the sound of his own voice more than he liked truth.

"My lady?"

Ettu's voice drew me from my musings and I realised she was still waiting for me to expand on my brief answer. I didn't want to reveal how foolish I had been.

"I don't know what I expected." It wasn't true, but she wouldn't know. "I suppose I might have thought more of him if he hadn't made us wait so long and then if his speech had…"

My voice trailed away as I realised it mightn't be wise to criticise the man Father had sent me halfway around the world to marry. Ettu gave me a hurt look and turned her attention to fussing over Ahmose, making sure the old woman was comfortable in her chair.

It wasn't that I didn't trust Ettu. Her stoic acceptance of the role of thief when Tiye's missing finger ring was discovered on her person told me clearer than anything else I could trust her. But I feared my dislike of Pharaoh revealed too much about my own character. Father had sent me to seal the alliance between Babylon and Egypt. That was my duty and it mattered little what the man he had offered me to was like. But I couldn't say this to Ettu. It wouldn't be a truthful representation of how I felt.

"Do you wish for me to go to Tall and Half tonight?" Ahmose asked, waving away Ettu's fussing. "I can try again to understand whatever it is Tall thinks you should know."

Careful! Pharaoh! Danger! That was the message he sent back with Ahmose last time. The warning was clear, although the nature of the danger still eluded us.

"You went out only last night. I think you should rest tonight." If Tall could tell her more, it would be valuable information. But Ahmose was an old woman — fifty years at least — and I couldn't expect her to spend every night wandering the streets of Thebes. "Besides, is it safe for you to use the potion so often?"

"I suppose if I start glowing in the dark, we can assume not," Ahmose said.

I laughed, surprised at her humour, although I didn't miss that she hadn't really answered my question. I would try to remember to ask her again, but in private. Maybe she didn't want to worry the others.

"I could go," Ettu said. "There might be news about Pharaoh's visit today. Someone should go to them as soon as possible."

I supposed they were all wondering the same as me: why Pharaoh hadn't yet summoned me to meet him. Had my Father done something to offend him? Had relations between Babylon and Egypt cooled to the point that Pharaoh didn't even want to meet the Babylonian princess sent to marry him? Would anyone tell me if the terms of the alliance had changed? Probably not.

"If anyone is to go, it should be me," Ahmose said.

One look at her wan face told me she didn't have the strength for another night so soon spent walking all the way to Pharaoh's palace and back.

"You can give me the potion ingredients and tell me what to do," Ettu said. "There is no reason it has to be you. There are three of us to share the burden."

She nodded towards Merytre, signalling it was she, and not me, who Ettu considered the third person. Merytre was swift to agree.

"It isn't hard, is it?" she asked. "You just have to see the guards' faces and then drink the potion, right? It worked for Ettu the time she went out."

"Well, yes," Ahmose said. "The knowledge is in the ingredients. Once the potion has been prepared, it should work for anyone."

"Could Tall and Half use it?" I asked. "If you prepared extra ingredients, could someone take it to them so they could come to us?"

Ahmose tapped her chin as she considered my questions.

"I don't see why not," she said. "As long as they don't mix it with water until they need it or it will lose its potency. But are they not more valuable to you in Pharaoh's palace?"

"I agree," Ettu said, although the look on her face said she was torn. I supposed she would like Half to be here. "They are our only source of information from the outside. We can trust nobody else to tell us the truth, rather than what the administrators want us to know."

"Merytre?" I asked. "What is your opinion?"

She hadn't met Tall or Half, but I wanted each of my companions to feel like their views mattered. We needed each other if we were to survive in this place. Merytre opened her mouth, but stopped and gave me a look that seemed filled with uncertainty.

"Go on," I said. "We should each have a say in such an important decision."

"If it is as Ettu says," Merytre said hesitantly, "that you can trust what they tell you, then I agree there is more value in leaving them where they are."

"But if there is any danger to them, we should retrieve them at once," Ettu said.

"How would we do that?" I asked. "So far, we can get a

message to them, but they have no way to send anything to us."

"Could we give them a code word?" Ettu suggested. "They could send a message to the Palace, something unimportant and uncontroversial which that scribe, Pentau, would have no reason to censor, but if they use the code word, we would know they are in danger and someone can go get them."

"What if Pentau doesn't pass the message on, regardless of its contents?" Merytre asked, seemingly emboldened now. After all, she was the one with the most experience in how the Palace functioned. "It is quite possible that any message from unknown men would not be forwarded."

"They could pretend the message was from my father," I said. "Perhaps with news from home. We could agree on something specific, like that my mother is ill, so if such a message arrives and it contains the agreed wording, I would know it isn't really from Father."

"Even that might not be passed onto you," Merytre said. "We have no way of knowing what Pentau would see fit to censor or withhold entirely."

"So how do we arrange for them to send us word if we can't trust that *any* message will be forwarded?" Ettu asked. "It seems the only solution is for them to use Ahmose's potion and come to us without warning. They would have to wait in the grounds somewhere and hope we find them before anyone else does."

I stared down at my hands as we pondered the problem. My nails were perfectly shaped, my skin smooth from the perfumed oils my ladies rubbed into my skin every day. I was more used to my nails being ragged and untended, always too busy as I was with learning and with a distaste of being fussed over by maids. These looked like the hands of a stranger.

Our musing was interrupted by a knock at the door. Ettu was quick to get to her feet and answer it.

"A visitor for Lady Kassaya," came the smooth voice of Panouk, the Palace's chief administrator.

Ettu's body shielded the visitor from my sight, so it wasn't until she thanked Panouk and ushered the woman into my chamber that I saw who it was. I stared at her for a long moment, too stunned to speak.

The woman gave me a shaky smile and burst into tears.

"Ishtar," I finally managed.

CHAPTER 2

My sister looked little like I remembered. She was skinnier and her belly, which surely should have been rounded with her child by now, was as flat as ever. Her face was pale and sad and tired, her eyes shadowed by dark circles.

My feet were rooted to the floor. Once, I would have gone to her immediately and wrapped my arms around her to soothe her as she cried. But bitterness swirled within me and I realised I hadn't yet forgiven her for her treachery.

"Why are you here?" My voice was cold and Ishtar cried even harder.

I smoothed my skirt, willing myself not to rise, despite my instinct to comfort her. I wouldn't go to her. I couldn't.

Ishtar dropped to her knees in front of me and lay her head on my lap.

"Dear sister," she said. "Father has sent me to be your maid."

"Why?"

Ishtar had always been his favourite. The beautiful one.

The elegant one. The one who could sing and dance and who Father would marry off into the most advantageous match. As angry as he was when she got herself with child to avoid being sent to Pharaoh, I had thought he would forgive her sooner or later. Father could never stay angry with Ishtar for long.

"The babe didn't live to be born," she whispered. She looked up at me for the briefest moment, then buried her face in my lap again. Her shoulders shook as she sobbed. "So Father sent me to you. He said that since I was supposed to go to Pharaoh, I may as well go anyway. I am to be one of your maids and to serve you as the others do."

She sat back on her heels, wiping the tears from her face, and looked around the chamber. She must have noticed the absence of Nammu and Belet-ili. Like Ettu, they used to be her maids, chosen by Ishtar herself and named for Babylonian goddesses as she was. She had been devastated that Father decided they would come with me to Egypt when I was sent in her place.

"Nammu is a snake," I said roughly. "And Belet-ili is little better."

Ishtar swallowed down her questions, although I could see she dearly wanted to ask where the women were. Nammu, in particular, she would want to see. She had always been close to Nammu. Closer than I had realised.

"I have as many lady's maids as I need." I had no real intention of sending her away — after all, where would she go? — but I wanted to hurt her like she had hurt me. "A full ten of them, plus Ahmose who is my tutor."

Ishtar burst into tears again.

"Please, Sister." She clasped her hands together, begging me as she looked up with tear-filled eyes. "Father has said I must serve you. I cannot go back. He will not have me in his court again. I am here alone. He would not even let me bring so much as a single maid."

"We do have a spare chamber, my lady," Ettu said.

A few minutes ago I had thought Tall and Half could share the spare chamber if they needed to flee Pharaoh's palace. I didn't want to give it to Ishtar.

"I suppose you can sleep in there for now." Ishtar would know from my voice how unwilling I was, but I was still too angry with her to try to hide it.

"Your palace is very fine." Ishtar wiped her face with her sleeve as she looked around. "It would seem Pharaoh was very pleased to have you as his wife."

I almost choked on the laugh that burst out of me.

"How did you even find me?" I asked. "Did you not go to Pharaoh's palace?"

"I did," she said. "I asked for you by name, but the guards didn't know who you were. When I said you were sent from Babylon to marry Pharaoh, they told me to come here. I didn't expect you to have your own palace. Pharaoh certainly favours you. Father would be most pleased."

I sniggered and she looked at me blankly, clearly confused by my reaction. Of course, she wouldn't yet understand what an Ornament was. It had taken me longer than this to understand the truth of my situation. It was only when Ettu returned that I realised she must have slipped away earlier.

"I have made the bed for you, Princess," she said to Ishtar. "Perhaps you would like to rest? I remember how weary I was after such a long journey."

"There is no need for you to call me that." Ishtar's tone was bitter now. "Father says I am no longer his daughter. I am no better than you, just another servant to my sister."

Ettu gave her a steady look. If she was at all surprised by

Ishtar's apparent demotion, or her acceptance of it, she didn't show it.

"Well then, Ishtar," she said. "I will show you to your bedchamber. Merytre, perhaps you could send for some hot water? I am sure Ishtar would like to bathe."

Ettu led Ishtar away and Merytre slipped out the door to find a runner boy. Ahmose and I looked at each other.

"Your sister, I gather," she said.

"My older sister. The one who was supposed to come here."

"I see."

Ahmose's face gave away little and I wondered what exactly it was she saw.

"I suppose our plan is unchanged?" she asked. "If Ettu is to go to Tall and Half tonight, I should prepare the ingredients for the potion."

I nodded and she too left, leaving me alone in the sitting chamber. Gone was the disappointment at discovering Pharaoh wasn't the man I had expected him to be. Gone, too, was my surprise at Ishtar's arrival. Now I felt only numbness.

When Ettu returned, she sank onto a couch and sighed.

"Well," she said. "That was unexpected."

"She is resting?" I couldn't think of what else to say.

"She was crying again," Ettu said. "I didn't know what to do, so I told her I would leave her to rest."

"I can't believe she's here."

How angry must Father have been to send her to Egypt? He was furious when she got herself with child, thus escaping her responsibility to the alliance. She must have known Father couldn't take back his promise to send a daughter to Pharaoh. Resentment filled me and already I regretted saying she could have the spare chamber.

So, I wasn't numb after all. I took a few deep breaths and tried to let go of my angry thoughts. Thinking about it again and again served no purpose. No matter how angry I was with her, Ishtar was still my sister, and whether she realised it or not, that meant I now had one more ally here.

CHAPTER 3

As dusk fell, Ettu drank the potion that would let her slip I past the gate guards unseen. She left with a sack containing the ingredients for another dose to get her into Pharaoh's palace if she needed it, and more to leave with Tall and Half in case they had to flee. The ingredients were small enough — mostly herbs, I assumed, although I guessed there might also be something more uncommon — but still the possibility that she might be caught with them on her made me uneasy.

We had identified a hidden spot within the Palace grounds where Ettu would tell Tall and Half to wait if they needed to come to us. Someone would check there every day. I had no idea how we would get them inside, but if they came, we would find a way. Sutem, one of the guards who patrolled the grounds, might possibly be persuaded to help, especially if Merytre was the one to ask him. There were an awful lot of ways it might go wrong, but none of it seemed beyond what we could manage, and we could use the jewels Father sent with me if we needed bribes.

The servants brought our evening meal and Ishtar's eyebrows rose at the amount of food they laid out for us. Even in Father's court, we didn't eat like this every night, with roasted meats and root vegetables, bread, cheeses, salad, and a variety of fruits. To drink, there was always wine, beer, and melon juice. As we ate, I told Ishtar a little about my situation.

"This palace is where Pharaoh's wives all live," I said.

"It is very big from what I saw." Ishtar's gaze was firmly on her plate as she poked at her food. She didn't react at my mention of multiple wives. So, that was no surprise to her. "There must be many servants to run such a large complex."

"He has many hundreds of wives." I hadn't yet forgotten my shock at learning such a thing and, perversely, I was pleased to see Ishtar was finally surprised.

"Hundreds?" she repeated, her voice incredulous. Her gaze flicked up briefly before she realised and fixed it firmly on her plate again. "But…"

Her voice trailed away and I waited to see if she would volunteer what she knew.

"You knew you wouldn't be queen," I said when she offered nothing else. "You knew there were other wives."

"I did," she admitted. "But I thought that meant three or four. I thought there was still…"

"Still what?" I prodded.

"Still the possibility you might be queen," she whispered. She met my eyes at last. "Sister, I am sorry I didn't tell you."

"You should have. I had no idea what I was coming to. I could have been more prepared."

"I know." Ishtar looked away. She seemed to have little appetite and had only picked at her food. I was relieved she had stopped crying, for now at least, but her face was still far too pale. Maybe she had been ill, or maybe she still grieved the loss of her babe. "When the guards said I must go to the Palace of the Ornaments, I truly thought it was your own residence. I thought it meant each of Pharaoh's wives had a palace of their own."

"Ornament is merely what the people here call Pharaoh's wives who are not his queen."

"So you have married him?" she asked. "Would you tell me about the ceremony? I suppose it must have been extravagant. Pharaoh is very wealthy from what Father told me."

"I haven't even met him." I had been so preoccupied with that fact, it hadn't occurred to me to wonder whether there would be any sort of ceremony. I supposed not. Surely a man who took so many wives didn't have time for a marriage ceremony with each of them.

"But you left Babylon well over two months ago," Ishtar said. "Does he not know you have arrived?"

It was startling to realise so little time had passed. Was it really only a couple of weeks since I arrived in Thebes? It felt like at least a year. Ishtar must have lost her babe very soon after I left. I supposed Father sent her to Egypt straight away. There was no reason for him to keep her anymore. As a maiden, she was of value to him. Even pregnant, she carried his grandchild. But now that she was neither? He couldn't marry her to someone else, so what use was she?

"Well?" Ishtar prodded.

"I have no idea."

She blinked at me and didn't seem to know what to say.

"I have had no communication with him," I said. "Apparently we only see him when he calls for us. In fact, I saw him for the first time only today. He came to give a speech and the Ornaments were all summoned to listen. I thought he might ask for me afterwards…"

My voice trailed away. I hadn't meant to tell her so much, but it was easy to fall into old habits of sharing intimate details with Ishtar.

"Father wouldn't have sent you here if he had known," she said.

I guessed what she was really thinking was that surely Father wouldn't have sent *her* to such a situation.

"I assume you have written to him," she continued. "You must have told him. I expect he will send for you to return home."

And her with me, of course.

"I wrote, but I doubt he will call me home," I said. "Regardless of whether he expected so many wives, he won't risk breaking the alliance. This is to prevent war between Babylon and Egypt. It is much bigger than the fate of one woman."

Ishtar opened her mouth but closed it again, the words left unsaid. I could see she wanted to argue with me, to tell me Father would take my happiness into account, but we both knew the truth. Father would do what was best for Babylon. It was what he always did. And that meant I would stay. I searched for something else to tell her, a way to change the subject. It hurt too much to think about how Babylon was more important to Father than I was.

"You remember Tall and Half?" I asked. "They came with me."

"The idiot and the halfwit," Ishtar said predictably.

"Don't call them that." I shot her a glare and she immediately lowered her gaze. "They are as intelligent as anyone else, and more so than many of the people I know."

"Of course," she murmured.

Ishtar would never have responded to me so meekly

before. She always had the last word. It was her right as the oldest.

"Tall and Half are living in Pharaoh's palace," I said. "They listen for things that might be useful for me."

"Like what?" Ishtar asked.

"When Ahmose saw them, they told her Pharaoh was planning to visit us here. I was able to get to the courtyard early and had a good view of him as he spoke."

"That's all?" She gave me a doubtful look.

"It mightn't sound like much, but that sort of information can be very useful. And that was just one conversation. That's where Ettu has gone tonight. To find out what else they have learned."

"Ettu?"

Of course, Ishtar wouldn't remember the name a maid had before she was re-named for a goddess. Perhaps she never asked their names at all.

"You called her Tiamat," I said. "Now that she is no longer in your service, she has chosen to use the name her father gave her."

Ishtar only nodded. Whatever feelings she had about this, she kept to herself.

"You should eat some more," I said. "You've hardly had anything yet and I remember how I longed for fresh food after being so long at sea."

"I cannot eat much." Ishtar looked down at the plate balanced on her knees. She had taken only a small portion of cheese and a few slices of cucumber, but I had seen her eat no more than a single bite. "Since the babe…"

Her voice trailed away and she swallowed hard. I didn't push her. Considering she had only gotten herself with child to avoid being sent to Egypt, she was taking the loss harder than I expected. As angry as I was with her still, I had no wish to distress her about the babe.

"You should try the baked fish," I said. "It's very tasty."

"You know I don't eat fish."

I had forgotten. She was sick once as a child after eating fish and had never eaten it again. Not knowing what else to do, I talked. I told her about Tiye's stolen jewels and how Nammu planted one of them in my clothing chest and then gave the other to Panouk, claiming to have found it in my chambers.

"Nammu would never do such a thing," Ishtar said. "She is as loyal a servant as I ever knew."

"To you, maybe," I said. "But she is still angry at being sent here without you and she seems to blame me for that, even though I wanted her to come as little as she did."

"You must be mistaken. Even if she was angry, Nammu wouldn't try to frame you for a theft you didn't commit. She must genuinely think you stole it, or that one of your servants did."

She stared down at her plate, as if willing herself not to look at Merytre or Ahmose.

I cleared my throat and debated how to handle such a comment.

"Ishtar," I said finally. "The women who live here in these chambers with me are those I trust completely. They have proved themselves to me in a way Nammu hasn't. I will hear no ill said of them. My willingness to allow you to stay here depends on this."

"Of course. Forgive me, Sister. I forgot my place."

I was already tired of her apparent humbleness. It was all pretence anyway. I knew Ishtar well enough to know she was merely waiting for an opportunity.

"Ishtar, I don't need you to act as a servant," I said. "If you stay here, I want you to be my sister, not another maid."

"Father sent me to serve you. He wrote to Pharaoh to explain, although I don't know how much he revealed about his reasons. He wouldn't want Pharaoh to know one of his daughters was so disobedient as to get herself with child to avoid doing what he required of her."

"Why did you do it?" I asked. "We grew up knowing Father would choose who we married. What was so terrible about coming here that you would do such a thing to avoid it?"

She stared down at her plate for a long time. She had given up even pretending to eat.

"It was too humiliating," she said at last. "To be sent off to another country, to marry its king, yes I expected that. But to know I wouldn't be queen? And that everyone would know it? No, I couldn't endure such a thing."

"Does Pharaoh know it was supposed to be you who came here, not me?" Despite my best intentions, my tone was bitter.

"I don't know."

"I doubt we will ever know then," I said. "He probably won't even remember by the time I meet him."

CHAPTER 4

As the evening grew late, I sent the others off to bed.

"You can't sit up all night again," Merytre protested. "I will wait for Ettu so you can sleep."

"I will sleep here on the couch," I said. "I want to know the moment she returns."

"I will wake you as soon as she is back."

Eventually, she realised I wouldn't be persuaded and went off to her bedchamber. I lay down and made myself comfortable. Ettu wouldn't be back for hours yet, so there was no point in staying awake.

I woke with a start. I had been dreaming, something dark and confusing about men coming into my chamber and dragging me out. I kicked and screamed but couldn't get away from them.

"My lady?" Ettu shook me again, harder this time.

I finally realised I was still on the couch. Safe in my chambers. My face was wet with tears and I clenched my fists so hard, my hands ached.

"I think you were dreaming," Ettu said. "I'm sorry if I startled you."

"Men." My chest was tight and I could hardly force out the words. "Taking me from my chambers."

"Hardly surprising you would dream about such a thing, given recent events."

She meant Nebtu's disappearance. Nobody had heard from her in more than a week, not even Henutmire who she was close to. The administrators said she had returned to her father's house, but there were whispers of other women who disappeared in the night just like Nebtu. Women who were never heard from again. The administrators always had a ready story. The woman had gone back to her family. She fled with a secret lover. She simply ran away. Nobody believed the stories, even if they weren't willing to say it. I sat up and wiped my face, trying to shake off the lingering memories of the nightmare.

"Did you find them?" I asked.

"I did and they have learned much. Let me get a drink and I will tell you."

"Sit," I said. "I can get it for you."

I got up too quickly and my head spun, sending me toppling back down onto the couch. Ettu had already poured herself some beer before I could get to my feet.

"Should I wake the others?" she asked.

"No, let them sleep."

I wanted to hear what she had learned before Ishtar did. With her here, I felt like I needed to be more guarded in my responses. Even if she hadn't come expecting to find me installed as queen, I wasn't ready for her to see how vulnerable I felt. I sat back down and prepared myself to hear whatever it was Ettu had learned.

"Firstly, Pharaoh has been advised of your arrival," she said.

"He has?" I had almost managed to convince myself he mustn't know. Surely he would have summoned me if he did.

"Tall overheard a conversation, but he could only tell me they were men. If he knew what positions they held, he didn't seem to have the words to express it."

It could be difficult to know whether Tall didn't know any more than he said, or if he just couldn't convey it. Ettu paused to sip her beer.

"He seemed to think Pharaoh had only recently been told, although I'm not sure he was certain of that," she continued.

"Go on."

"After the big speech yesterday, Tiye was summoned. She spent the evening with Pharaoh."

"Is that information from Tall as well?"

"No, Half. From what he heard, she was the only Ornament Pharaoh spent time with while he was here."

"I suppose I shouldn't be offended then." She was his favourite, after all.

"He sees Tiye almost every week. Sometimes he also sees one or two other women when he visits."

And yet, not me. How many times had he come to the Palace since I arrived? He had supposedly been away at a religious festival in Dendera, so maybe it wasn't many.

"How does Half know this?" I asked.

She shrugged. "There wasn't time to ask for details. By the time I walked all the way there and found them, we could only speak for a few minutes before I had to start back. I couldn't risk the potion wearing off before I got back inside the gates. I didn't want to take the other dose unless I had to."

"Is there anything else?"

"I told them about the stolen jewels," she continued. "Half will listen for any rumours. It would be useful for us to know what folk say about you."

"You left the rest of the ingredients with them?"

"Yes, and I explained how to use the potion. Half said they will come if they have reason to flee, but he thought they could best serve you by staying where they are."

It was true, but I would have preferred to know all my allies were safe within the walls of the Palace of the Ornaments.

"There is just one other piece of news." Ettu drained the last of her beer and set the mug aside. "Half said a servant disappeared from Pharaoh's palace a couple of months ago, not long before we arrived. A woman."

"Disappeared like Nebtu?"

"Yes, although the servants there are allowed to come and go as they wish. Apparently she worked late one night and then never came back the next day."

"Nobody saw her leave that night?"

She shook her head.

"So it is not only here that women disappear from," I said. Absently, I wondered at my lack of surprise. Perhaps I had somehow known the issue was bigger than we suspected, even if I hadn't let myself think it.

"There must be a connection," she said. "Maybe a servant who works at both locations. Or a messenger, or someone who delivers goods. There are surely many people who have access to both palaces."

"To do what? Abduct a woman? Drag her out kicking and screaming?"

The memory of my nightmare rose up again and my chest

tightened. I pushed the images away. It was a dream and nothing more.

"Somebody knows what has happened," Ettu said. "Half will find out what he can."

"The last thing we need is for him to draw attention to himself snooping around."

"He will be careful. He won't do anything to jeopardise their position in Pharaoh's palace. He is aware of how valuable that is to you."

"I don't want him doing anything to jeopardise his own safety either. There's more at stake than our ability to get covert news from the palace."

"You don't need to worry. If there is even the slightest hint of danger to themselves, they will flee. I was very stern with them about it. And remember, folk aren't stopped from leaving Pharaoh's palace. Half and Tall can walk right out any time they want."

I had only been here a couple of weeks, but already such freedom seemed incredible.

CHAPTER 5

I couldn't get back to sleep after Ettu's return. It was almost dawn anyway and I had planned to go to Tiye's chambers this morning. Although I had promised we would sit together and talk, I hadn't yet found time to do so. This regular meeting was supposed to be both a cover for the fact that I wasn't really cleaning her bathing chamber and also a chance to fulfil my promise to her: to be a friend. But given the recent uproar around her stolen jewels, the matter suddenly seemed urgent. I needed to make sure she didn't believe Nammu's story that I was the thief.

I suffered the usual indignity of being stripped naked, bathed and shaved, before my lady's maids dressed me. I sat on a stool as they made up my face and arranged the wig Ettu had selected. Belet-ili spotted Ishtar straight away and they greeted each other with hugs. I watched as they talked, their heads close together, and wished I could hear what they said. No doubt Belet-ili gave her own version of the affair of the stolen jewels. Who would Ishtar believe? Her sister or a once-favoured maid?

They seem to argue at one point, although their voices were too low for me to hear anything. Ishtar went to the window and stood looking out, her arms crossed over her chest. I couldn't tell whether she was angry or upset. Belet-ili followed her, talking earnestly, and I wished the chattering maids around me would be quiet so I might catch some of their conversation.

At last I was attired to their satisfaction and my maids left, Belet-ili with them. She and Ishtar hugged again before she departed. So whatever they had argued about, it seemed they had made up. I left to break my fast in the dining chamber, taking only Ettu with me. I suggested she stay behind and rest, but she insisted she wasn't too tired to accompany me.

"Did you hear anything of what they said?" I asked quietly as we walked. There were more folk around than usual today, despite the early hour.

"No, although I tried," Ettu said. "They were being careful to make sure nobody overheard them."

"What do you think Belet-ili was saying to her?"

Ettu shrugged and seemed unwilling to speculate. I supposed that was fair enough. She knew no more than I did.

In the dining chamber, the air buzzed with suppressed excitement. I claimed the table beside Henutmire and she nodded at me in greeting. Ettu straightened my skirt so it wouldn't crease while I was sitting, then went to stand against the wall with the other maids. Henutmire and I said nothing as the serving women came to present their trays to me.

"So," Henutmire said as the last of the serving women left. "Was yesterday the first time you saw Pharaoh?"

"It was." I took a bite of bread before she could ask my opinion of him. It was dense and tasty, even without honey.

"And what did you think?" she asked. "Is he not handsome?"

I made a show of chewing to give myself time to think. Handsome was not a word I would have used. He might have been once, many banquets ago, but his pompous tone and arrogant words made it hard for me to find anything attractive about him.

"He seems to have a very strong personality," I said at last. It was the kindest thought I could find that didn't feel like a lie.

"He has bedded me twice." Henutmire's voice was pitched low as if this was a confession.

"How long have you been here?"

"Almost four years."

Twice in four years? I supposed she hadn't borne him a babe, but I couldn't think of the right way to ask. Perhaps she didn't want to give him sons anyway, or perhaps she did and the reminder she had failed would be cruel.

"Is there any news on Nebtu?" I asked, hoping she would forget I had given no other opinion on Pharaoh.

Henutmire sighed and shook her head. She toyed with a small pile of dates on her plate, but didn't seem to be eating much.

"Nothing and I don't expect there will be anything. There never is in these cases. I have tried to send messages to her family, but I know Pentau won't forward them. I don't even know why I bother."

I paused to think carefully before I spoke. My instincts said I could trust Henutmire. If I could be useful to her, I might make another ally. I made sure there were no servants within earshot.

"I might have a way of getting a message out," I whispered.

She gave me a surprised look.

"Surely you have been here long enough to know how such things work," she whispered back. "Only the messages Pentau approves will be sent."

"Write a letter and I will get it out if I can. You can give it to Ettu, my lady's maid who is standing just over there. You can trust her."

Henutmire eyed me, as if wondering whether she could trust me. I supposed the level of competition amongst the Ornaments must mean the women played all sorts of games with each other.

"I have no interest in playing the games of the Palace," I said. "Nebtu's family should know she is missing. That is my only concern."

At length, she nodded.

"I will give your maid my letter today," she said. "I will place it in her hand myself."

"I will tell her to expect it."

We finished our meal in silence and I gave Henutmire a nod as I rose to leave. Ettu rushed over to straighten my gown and we left.

"Henutmire will give you a letter for Nebtu's family," I said quietly as we headed towards Tiye's chambers.

"You told her you could get a message out? Was that wise?"

"I think we can trust her. She and Nebtu were friends, and she seems to be the only person here who is genuinely concerned about her."

We reached the hallway leading to Tiye's suite and I allowed Ettu to smooth my wig and straighten my gown again, although they surely didn't need any adjustment when all I had done was walk through the Palace.

"Should I wait here for you?" Ettu asked.

"Go get some sleep. You have been out all night."

When I knocked on Tiye's door, it was Nammu who answered. She looked me up and down, then sneered.

"Do you have an appointment?" she asked snidely.

"As a matter of fact, I do." My voice was steady. I didn't intend to let Nammu see how much it discomfited me to realise she would be in the chamber while I visited with Tiye. How could we discuss Nammu's lies about the stolen jewels with her there to listen? "Tell your *mistress* I am here."

I emphasised the word, wanting her to know I hadn't forgotten her betrayal.

The door closed in my face. I waited. This seemed to be usual with Tiye's maids. The door opened again and Nammu gestured for me to enter.

"Please come in." Her voice was more contrite this time and I wondered whether Tiye had rebuked her for how she greeted me.

Tiye lounged on a couch, dressed as if she waited to meet with Pharaoh himself. And perhaps she was. I had no doubt she knew before anyone else when he was due to visit.

"So." Tiye raised her eyebrows at me. "I thought you had forgotten your promise."

"I'm sorry it has taken me so long to come."

I sat on the couch facing hers without waiting for an invitation. If I waited politely, she would probably keep me standing there for the sake of making me feel uncomfortable. I smoothed my skirt over my knees and tried to give the appearance of being at ease.

"Refreshments?" Tiye asked. "Nammu, go fetch a fresh jug of melon juice."

"The one there on the table was only delivered a few minutes ago," Nammu said. She had already sat herself down on a chair in the corner of the chamber and made no move to rise.

Tiye said nothing, only looked steadily at her.

"Of course," Nammu said quickly. She left.

Tiye and I exchanged a look.

"She is a difficult one," she said to me.

"And yet you chose to take her on. After the trouble she caused, did you expect anything else?"

"No, I suppose not."

She said nothing further and I wondered whether she waited for an explanation from me.

"I didn't steal your jewels," I said. "We are allies, but even if we weren't, I am no thief."

"No," she said. "I didn't think you were. You are too direct to do such a thing. If you wanted one of my jewels, I expect you would take it right in front of me."

She had misjudged me, but I didn't correct her. Let her think such a thing if she wanted. It was to my advantage anyway.

"Then why give Nammu a position?" I asked. "You must surely realise she is the one most likely to be the thief."

"Oh, I know she is." Tiye raised her eyebrows at me, seemingly amused. "One of my lady's maids encountered her leaving my chambers. She snuck in when nobody was around. When my maid confronted her, she claimed you had sent her with a message for me and she was merely trying to deliver it."

"Then why did you report the jewels as stolen, but without saying you knew who the thief was?"

"I wanted to understand her plan. A woman like that doesn't steal a jewel simply because it is beautiful and she desires it for herself. No, she had a plan and I wanted to know what it was."

"My maid, Ettu, could have been imprisoned, or worse. She was the one who found the jewel Nammu hid in my clothing chest and she still had it on her when Panouk searched my chambers."

Tiye shrugged, as if to say the life of a servant was of no concern to her.

"Surely you didn't need to offer her a position," I said. "To reward her for her lies and deception."

"A servant like her, one who is willing to cause so much havoc, could be useful," Tiye said. "Especially if she is loyal."

"I am not sure that Nammu is loyal to anyone other than herself."

Except my sister. She had been loyal to Ishtar.

"Perhaps you simply don't know how to make her loyal," she said.

"And you do?"

Tiye gave me a tight smile. "We shall see, shan't we?"

"So we are still allies?" I eyed her, wondering whether she toyed with me the same way she did with Nammu.

"Of course." Tiye gave me a bemused look. "As long as you fulfil your side of our agreement."

"I intend to."

"I hear there are two Babylonian men recently installed within Pharaoh's palace." She tipped her head to the side as she studied me. "Companions of yours, I assume? The timing suggests they must have arrived with you."

"Two of my attendants. They travelled with me, but they weren't allowed to stay. Amankhau turned them out, despite telling me they could sleep in the stables."

"You are fortunate they weren't executed on the spot for entering the grounds."

"I would not have stood for that."

"Hmm."

She didn't seem inclined to offer anything further about Tall and Half.

"How did you hear about them?" I asked.

"Pharaoh mentioned them last night." She stretched, all elegant casualness now. "He finds them amusing, the short one in particular."

"His name is Half."

"Pharaoh couldn't remember. He calls him the little funny fellow."

"I'm pleased they are making themselves useful."

I longed to know if Pharaoh had said anything else about them, but didn't want to sound too eager. I supposed that from Tiye's point of view, they were servants and of little interest.

"It would be useful to have servants you can trust in Pharaoh's palace," Tiye said.

"It would be if there was a way of communicating with them."

My heart hammered. Surely she didn't suspect? How could she know such a thing?

"Hmm," was all she said.

I suspected that sound probably meant more than it implied.

"Have you heard about Nebtu?" I asked. "Nobody has seen her in more than a week."

"Yes, a very unpleasant situation." Tiye frowned and looked genuinely concerned.

"Is Pharaoh aware? The administrators don't seem to be doing anything to find her, but Pharaoh could launch a proper investigation."

Tiye's concern vanished, replaced with the cool, blank expression I was more familiar with.

"I wouldn't know," she said. "We don't discuss such things. When he wants to spend time with me, it is because he needs to relax. I don't talk about anything that might distress him."

"But surely he would want to know an Ornament is missing?"

She pursed her lips and looked away. So if anyone was going to tell Pharaoh, it clearly wouldn't be Tiye.

The door opened and Nammu returned with a jug. She poured a mug of juice for Tiye, then set the jug on a side table. Tiye cleared her throat and gave her a pointed look, and Nammu swiftly poured a mug for me as well. I set it aside without tasting it.

"I must go," I said, getting to my feet. "I will come back again in a day or two."

Tiye nodded.

"See that you do," she said. "And don't wait so long next time."

CHAPTER 6

The door to my chambers flung open before I could touch the handle.

"I thought you would never return," Ettu said. "Come inside, quickly."

"What is it? Is it Tall and Half?"

She said nothing until the door was closed. My heart pounded as I waited. Ahmose sat on a couch, displaying none of the agitation Ettu did. Merytre and Ishtar were nowhere to be seen.

"You have a message from Pharaoh," Ettu said.

I finally noticed the scroll in her hand.

"What does it say?" I asked.

"I can't read Egyptian myself," she said.

But the look on her face said she knew the letter's contents.

"I'm guessing Ahmose can, though," I said. "So I assume the letter has been read."

Ahmose's face bore a contrite expression, but I waved away the apology before she could say it.

"I have no secrets," I said. "Tell me what it says."

"Go on then," Ettu said to Ahmose. "It should be you who tells her."

"Pharaoh will visit tonight and he has summoned you to dine with him," Ahmose said.

"Finally," I muttered.

The news didn't carry the same excitement as it would have before his big speech. Now, my only hope was that he would be different in private. Maybe the man we saw in the courtyard was his public persona, the king he thought people expected to see. He might be more pleasant than he seemed. Less pompous.

"I have chosen a gown for you," Ettu said. "Merytre and Ishtar have gone to find sewers to adjust it before tonight. I have also laid out a wig and jewels. Would you like to see them?"

"No, I am sure whatever you have selected is fine."

I dropped onto a couch, suddenly weary. The meeting with Tiye had been exhausting, feeling as I did that I needed to look for hidden meanings behind everything she said and be careful what I said myself. I supposed my dinner with Pharaoh would be no different.

"You should rest before then," Ettu said, as if sensing my fatigue. "I am sure you didn't sleep much last night since you were waiting on the couch when I got back."

"Should I mention Tall and Half to Pharaoh? Maybe he will be more inclined to allow them to stay if I speak for them."

"Do you think it is wise for him to know their connection to you?" Ettu asked. "It might have the opposite effect if he thinks you have sent them to spy on him."

What exactly had Tiye said about them? She knew they

were Babylonian, and she had guessed they arrived with me, but did she say Pharaoh knew too? My thoughts seemed to drift and I leaned back against the couch.

"Ahmose, what do you think?" I closed my eyes. Not to sleep, just to rest for a few moments.

I woke to the sound of a closing door, tearing me from another dream in which men dragged me from my chambers. Ishtar and Merytre had returned with two women I didn't recognise. The last thing I remembered was my question to Ahmose. If she replied, I never heard her and I couldn't ask again in front of the sewers. Ettu brought the gown she had selected — a strapless white sheath with a diaphanous, white overlay.

"It is very plain," I said. "Are you sure I should wear that?"

"This is the height of fashion," Merytre said.

"It is simple, but stylish," Ettu said. "I think you should look as Pharaoh expects his Ornaments to. For this first visit, at least. Perhaps after that you could dress in your usual style, but for now, I think you need to look like everyone else. Remind him you are an Ornament."

I held my tongue as they dressed me. I wouldn't have expected to wear one of my Babylonian gowns, but I had thought they would choose something more elaborate. The sewers planned their alterations, pinning the bust where they intended to adjust it to sit in a more flattering way. The gown was a little too short and they talked of adding an embroidered strip to the hem. I couldn't see that it mattered, but they fretted over every detail. At last, the sewers were satisfied and left, taking the gown with them and promising to return it in a few hours.

Ishtar stayed by the door while the sewers fussed over my dress. I had never seen her look uncertain before. Of the two of us, she had always been the more confident. But now it seemed it was me who felt more assured of my place here and she who didn't quite know what to do.

"What do you think of the Palace of the Ornaments?" I asked. Maybe she would feel more at ease if I made an effort to include her.

"It is very big," she said. "I thought Father's palace was big, but this..." Her voice trailed away.

"I suppose it needs to be enormous given how many residents it has."

I regretted it as soon as I said it. It was mean of me, really, to make a point yet again of how I was just one wife amongst many. A reminder this was the fate Father had intended to send her to, and that she hadn't warned me. Ishtar flinched a little and I knew she had understood my message.

"I don't think I would have found my way back to your chambers if Merytre hadn't been with me," she said. "We didn't go all that far, but I was already hopelessly lost."

She gave a little laugh and Merytre laughed with her. Irritation prickled at me. She wasn't supposed to be friendly with Merytre. She was supposed to be helpless and alone and totally dependant on me. That was why Father sent her here. He tore her from everything she knew and sent her to a foreign land to be a servant.

Just as he did with you, something inside me whispered. You might be the one with the maids and the jewels and the beautiful gowns, but never forget you are no less a servant than any other woman in this room. I forced a smile at Ishtar.

"You will find your way around soon enough," I said. "I am sure everyone will be pleased to help you."

Merytre gave an enthusiastic nod. Ettu agreed, but she

looked more cautious. Of course, she knew Ishtar better than Merytre did. Perhaps even better than me.

"Who do you wish to accompany you tonight, my lady?" Merytre asked.

"How many should I take with me?" I asked.

She frowned as she thought.

"The Ornaments I served previously took one, or maybe two, maids with them when they met with Pharaoh," she said. "Never me, though."

"I will take two then," I said. "You and Ishtar."

The words were out of my mouth before I realised what I was going to say, but it was too late to take them back. Why in Marduk's name did I say that? I didn't want to take Ishtar. She was the beautiful one. The elegant one. The one who was supposed to come here and marry Pharaoh. I didn't want him to see her for the first time in the same moment as he saw me.

"Of course." If Merytre thought my choice was unwise, her voice gave no hint of it.

If I hadn't been looking at Ishtar at just the right moment, I wouldn't have seen the expression that flashed across her face. She didn't look surprised I had chosen her. She looked hopeful.

CHAPTER 7

*E*ttu was grumbling about the sewers' lateness long before they returned my gown. I myself was too busy to worry about it, occupied as I was with being bathed and scrubbed and shaved by my entire team of maids, although surely no hair could have grown in the hours since they last shaved me this morning.

Ettu had insisted it would take all my maids to prepare me for my presentation to Pharaoh. I objected, preferring she and Merytre dress me themselves, until Ettu reminded me that the more women who saw me preparing to meet with Pharaoh, the faster word would go around. Everyone should know I had met him. It showed I was now somebody to take note of. Apparently some Ornaments hadn't met with Pharaoh even a year after their arrival.

Ettu introduced Ishtar to the others, giving only her name and the fact that she was newly arrived. Ishtar hung back while the women worked on me and the next time I looked for her, she was gone. I didn't comment on her absence, although I wondered where she was.

The women finally left, but not without many well wishes for the evening. It was only after they were gone that Ishtar reappeared. She had changed and made up her face. Her Babylonian tunic with its colourful fringe hanging from the hem and her hair pinned up behind her head emphasised her exotic beauty, and I wished again I hadn't said she could come. I didn't even know why I said it.

For a moment, I had wanted to share this occasion with her. I thought the knowledge that my sister stood behind me might make me feel more confident as I met the man who would dictate the rest of my life. But her beauty and her elegant gown made me feel underdressed in my simple shift, even though Merytre had insisted it was fashionable. Instead of the confidence of my sister's presence, I was painfully aware of how much more beautiful than me she was, and of how awkward I felt beside her.

"Well, then," I said. "I suppose I should leave."

Ettu started to raise her arms, as if she meant to hug me, but caught herself.

"Good luck," she said. "We will wait up for you."

"Don't," I said. "You and Ahmose both need some sleep. I might not be back until late."

Would Pharaoh expect me to spend the night with him? My heart suddenly pounded and my palms were sweating. Surely he wouldn't try to get me with child the first time he met me? *Show Pharaoh what the women of Babylon are made of.* Mother's words echoed through my mind. She would tell me to do my duty, regardless of how I felt about it. This was why I was here, after all. Father told me to bear many sons for Pharaoh. He would not expect I would have to be reminded to do my duty when the time came.

Merytre was already holding the door open for me. Ettu

darted forward to make one last adjustment to my wig and then I left, with Ishtar and Merytre at my heels.

Striding down the hallway, I felt like I was in some strange new version of the world I had become used to. The hallways were no less busy, but people moved aside to let me pass in a way they didn't usually. It seemed word had indeed gone around that I was to dine with Pharaoh tonight. I met nobody's eyes, but fixed my gaze straight ahead and tried not to notice the mutters as I passed. Were they speculating on my evening with Pharaoh or did they still gossip about my supposed theft of Tiye's jewels?

The footsteps of the two women behind me were soft, but every now and then a sandal scuffed against the mud brick floor. How strange that Ishtar was now my maid. Ishtar, the one who was supposed to make the most desirable marriage. Ishtar, my older sister.

"To the left, my lady," Merytre said when I paused at a spot where the hallway branched in two directions. "It is not much further."

"Tell me what I should expect," I said.

"You should prostrate yourself before him when he arrives. Don't get up until he tells you to, no matter how long he leaves you waiting. If he offers you his hand, he expects you to kiss it. I have heard he likes to be flattered, so you should praise him, if you can. If he wants conversation, you should focus all talk on him. He is unlikely to want to hear about you."

I longed to ask whether Pharaoh might expect to bed me tonight, but didn't have the courage, not with Ishtar there to hear me. Strange how I felt less comfortable showing my inexperience in front of her than my maids. My other maids.

I knew when we turned down the hallway leading to my

destination because a full squad of ten guards lined our path. They were fit and muscular, dressed in the white *shendyt* and sandals I had become accustomed to seeing on Egyptian men. Each carried a spear and had a dagger stuck through his waistband. So the prohibition against weapons inside the Palace obviously didn't apply to Pharaoh's own guards. I guessed the rule about modified men also didn't apply.

I might have expected them to stare straight ahead as I passed, but they didn't. I felt their gazes as they examined me and I wondered what they looked for. Were they judging whether I was beautiful enough to be an Ornament? Had they already decided whether I was to Pharaoh's taste? Did they inspect me and then turn their attention to Ishtar?

The guards on either side of the closed door watched as I approached. I stopped just in front of them and waited. Was I supposed to introduce myself? Surely they were expecting me. My nose tingled from the jasmine-scented oil that covered every bit of my skin and I tried not to sniffle. From behind me, Merytre spoke.

"Lady Kassaya, Princess of Babylon," she said. "Come to dine with Pharaoh at his command."

One of the guards stepped forward.

"I will need to search you for weapons, my lady," he said.

"Of course."

How did they think I would obtain any weapons? And where would I hide them, given the thinness of the fabric I wore? My heart pounded as he ran his hands over my body. I had never been so intimately touched by a man. My cheeks flushed and I hoped it wouldn't be noticeable in the flickering torch light. His search of me was thorough, but at last he stepped back and opened the door.

"My lady." He gestured for me to enter.

He searched Merytre and Ishtar too before they were allowed to follow me.

I had expected opulence and I wasn't disappointed. Soft rugs covered the mud brick floor. Small, low tables dotted the room, each with a fat cushion beside it. A bench along one wall bore a pair of jugs, several bottles of wine, and an assortment of goblets and plates. Several couches stood against another wall — each big enough for two or three people to sit together — and heavy shutters shielded the windows. Lamps on every available surface shed glittering light over the chamber, far too bright, and heated the air uncomfortably. Already, I sweated so much I worried the dampness would seep right through the delicate linen I wore.

The walls were covered with painted murals, the strange half-human, half-beast depictions of the gods that still seemed foreign to me no matter how many times I saw them. A man with the head of some kind of dog, several with bird heads, a strangely elongated naked woman who balanced on her hands and feet, her body arched over a much smaller man who looked like he was trying to suckle her breast. I understood none of them.

Pharaoh hadn't yet arrived. I wasn't surprised to realise he would keep me waiting.

"What should I do while I wait?" I whispered to Merytre. "Do I sit down?"

Before she could reply, the door opened and a serving woman entered. My cheeks heated at the sight of her, for she was almost entirely naked with nothing more than a woven girdle around her waist and golden chains around her neck and ankles.

"Wine, my lady?" she asked.

I looked away at the strange gods to avoid her nakedness.

"Please." At least it would give me something to do with my hands.

She poured from a wine bottle and handed me the goblet. It was a mellow red wine and I sipped it as I wandered around the chamber, examining the perplexing murals. Merytre and Ishtar had taken up positions against the wall, looking strangely conservative, fully dressed as they were, next to the serving woman. They made an odd-looking pair, with Ishtar in her Babylonian attire and Merytre wearing a simple shift that was not all that much different from mine.

I sipped my wine sparingly, not wanting a full bladder to distract me when Pharaoh finally arrived. A long time passed before the door to the hallway opened and a pair of guards entered. They moved around the room, seemingly examining everything, even though there was nowhere an intruder could possibly hide. One of them gave me a hard look and I braced myself, expecting to be searched again, but he returned to the doorway without touching me.

"My lord," he said.

Pharaoh swept in. His jowls wobbled and his linen shirt did nothing to disguise the bulbous belly that hung well over the waistband of his *shendyt*. He looked just as I remembered, except for his wig, an odd-looking thing, to my eye at least, with a shorter curly section over his scalp and longer braids of an entirely different colour. Being this close to him, I realised he was older than I had thought. He must be sixty years, at least. A broad collar made of tiny blue beads set in an intricate geometric design hung around his neck and every finger was laden with silver or gold finger rings. A silver circlet perched on his wig, an ostentatious statement of his importance, given this was supposed to be a private dinner for two.

"Wine," he called, ignoring me.

He collapsed onto a couch with a loud groan. Several more mostly-naked women hurried in from an adjoining chamber, one bearing a low footstool, which she rushed to place under Pharaoh's sandalled feet. It was only when he had a goblet in his hand that he even looked at me.

"The newest Ornament, I presume," he said.

I dropped to my knees in front of him, set my goblet on the floor, and lay on my belly. The rug beneath me was soft and clean, but its fibres made my already-irritated nose itch and I longed to turn my head to the side. Mindful of Merytre's instructions, I didn't dare move.

"And who might you be?" he asked, suddenly.

With my face pressed to the rug, I couldn't see who he spoke to, but I could guess even before she replied.

"My lord, I am Ishtar. I am lady's maid to my sister, Kassaya."

"Come sit beside me, Ishtar," he said, then more loudly, "fetch her some wine."

Ishtar's footsteps were no more than a whisper against the rugs as she crossed the chamber to prostrate herself beside me.

"Yes, yes." Pharaoh's tone was impatient now. "You can get up."

I got to my feet, snatching up my goblet as I rose. He probably meant only Ishtar, but I could pretend I thought he meant both of us. Marduk damn him, but I wasn't going to spend the evening lying on my belly while he courted my sister.

"My lord, I am Kassaya, sent to you by my father, King Marduk-apla-iddina of Babylon," I said.

"And why did Marduk-apla-iddina send you and not your

sister to me?" Pharaoh's gaze never left Ishtar as he took a gulp from his goblet.

"I do not presume to understand my father's motivations."

It took an effort to make my voice sound unconcerned. Did he not realise how rude he was being, or did he simply not care?

A servant handed Ishtar a goblet and she took it without even a thank you. When I glanced sideways at her, her gaze was on the floor and an attractive blush coloured her cheeks. Pharaoh patted the couch beside him and she went to sit there. He took up so much of the couch that she had to sit a little too close to him.

"My lord, I am here to seal the alliance between Babylon and Egypt," I said, determined to bring his attention back to me.

"And why are you here, my dear?" he asked Ishtar, his hand already stroking her knee.

"My father thought I would learn humility by serving my sister," Ishtar said.

"Humility is a very important quality for a woman to have." Pharaoh drained his goblet and held it out to be refilled without once taking his gaze off Ishtar. "Did you know I am a living god? Yes, that's right, you share a couch with a god. Think what an honour it would be to bear a son for a god."

Did he seriously intend to proposition Ishtar right in front of me?

"It was a very long journey from Babylon," I said. "And of course, when we first arrived in Egypt, I didn't realise that wouldn't be the end of our travels. Nobody told me you lived so far down the river."

It was a daft thing to say, but I doubted he heard me. He leaned close to Ishtar to whisper in her ear, his hand now high on her thigh. She giggled and blushed even more at whatever he whispered.

"My lord," I said, louder now.

He held out his goblet in my direction. When I didn't move, he finally dragged his gaze from Ishtar. He frowned at me.

"Wine," he said loudly and shook the goblet.

I only looked at him. A serving woman rushed to take the goblet from him. Once his hand was empty, he fluttered his fingers in my direction.

"Yes, yes," he said. "You can go."

Then he turned back to Ishtar.

CHAPTER 8

I gaped at Pharaoh, but his attention, brief as it had been, was already gone. I shot a desperate look towards Merytre who still stood against the wall where Ishtar should have been, but she shrugged. Not knowing what else to do, I went to her.

"Does he really expect me to leave while he fawns over Ishtar?" I whispered.

She tipped her head towards the door and together, we left. It was only once we were well down the hallway and out of earshot of the guards that she spoke.

"Oh, my lady," she said. "That was appalling."

"I didn't know what to do."

"I'm sure I wouldn't have either."

"That's Ishtar's particular talent. Drawing the attention of every man in the room." Resentment rose up within me again. How many times would Ishtar interfere in my life?

"Don't blame her, my lady. Her beauty is not her fault." She seemed to reconsider her words and shot me an apologetic look. "I don't mean—"

I waved away her apology, only now realising I still held my goblet. I certainly wasn't going to take it back.

"I know I'm not as beautiful as she is." My voice was bitter even as I tried to tell myself this was nothing new. "My whole life, I have been told how beautiful Ishtar is. How she will make the best marriage. It's hardly a surprise that Pharaoh prefers her to me."

"Why did your father send you instead of her? If she was supposed to make the best marriage, what did he intend for her when he sent you here?"

Merytre was there when Ishtar told me she had lost the babe, but I supposed her explanation mightn't have made much sense to anyone who wasn't already familiar with the situation.

"She was supposed to come," I said. "But she got herself with child to avoid it. Father had to send someone and I am his only other daughter."

"Oh." She was silent for a few moments, digesting this. "So you never expected to be sent away to marry?"

"I expected to spend the rest of my life in Babylon. I always knew Father would choose my husband, but since I'm not as pretty or as talented as Ishtar, I thought it would be a Babylonian noble. Someone whose support Father needed. Someone he wanted to keep close to him. I only found out I was to come to Egypt the day before I left."

"That must have been a terrible shock."

"It was. And when I left, I never thought to see Ishtar again. I suppose she is of no use to Father now."

Or was this some game Father played? If he knew I was to be an Ornament rather than queen, did he send Ishtar to me with the hope she would attract Pharaoh's attention? Did he think to have both his daughters bear sons for Pharaoh? Or did he consider me so unattractive that he sent Ishtar so he could be sure Pharaoh would want to bed at least one Princess of Babylon? I couldn't bear to think Father might be so cruel and I desperately wished I understood his reasons.

Ettu was waiting for us in the sitting chamber, despite my instruction for her to go to bed. Most of the lamps had been doused and only the one beside her still burned, welcoming me into this space of privacy and peace.

"My lady, you are back early." Ettu rubbed her eyes and got to her feet. "Where is Ishtar?"

She stopped and took a harder look at me. From the corner of my eye, I saw Merytre shake her head.

"Have you eaten?" Ettu's voice was brisker now. She didn't wait for a reply. "Sit and I'll put something together for you. They brought as much as ever, although they surely knew you wouldn't be here. There is roasted pig tonight, and three kinds of salad."

She chattered as she loaded a plate for me — some gossip she had heard, although it must have been clear I wasn't listening. Merytre poured me some melon juice and brought a bowl of water to wash my feet, even though they couldn't have been dirty after doing no more than walking through the Palace in my sandals.

My stomach felt too unsettled to eat, so I sipped the juice. At least it gave me a reason not to speak. When I finally looked back at Ettu, she raised her eyebrows at me, a reminder I hadn't yet offered any explanation for why Merytre and I were back so soon and without Ishtar.

"Ishtar is still with Pharaoh," I said.

"I see." Ettu's face showed she definitely did understand. Of course, she had served Ishtar for several years. Ettu knew what she was like.

"He seemed to take quite a liking to her," Merytre offered.

"As would be expected." For some reason, I suddenly felt like I had to defend Ishtar. "She is very beautiful, after all."

"But you are no less beautiful," Ettu said.

"You don't need to say such a thing." I picked at the food on my plate, although my appetite had fled.

"It is true," she said. "You see yourself in the hand mirror every day. Haven't you noticed your own beauty? It is different to Ishtar's, I'll admit, but you are beautiful none-theless."

"It isn't hard to see the two of you are sisters," Merytre said. "You look very much like each other."

"Now you're being ridiculous," I said. "I look nothing like Ishtar, other than that we both have dark hair and dark eyes."

"If you can't see it, then I don't know what else to say," Ettu said. "Other than to suggest you take a harder look in the hand mirror next time. But regardless of that, what do you intend to do about her?"

"Do?" I asked.

"She is supposed to be your servant, is she not?" Ettu said. "And yet she ruined your evening with Pharaoh."

"It was hardly her fault." I took a little bite of the roasted pig, but although it was tasty, I really didn't want it. "Pharaoh took one look at her and was besotted. He told her to sit with him and then he completely ignored me."

"Maybe next time Pharaoh calls for you, she should stay here," she said.

"If there is a next time," I said gloomily. I set my plate aside, even though I had barely touched the food. How angry would Father be if I failed to give Pharaoh a son? "He never even noticed me once he saw her. In fact, he told me to pour his wine, as if I was a servant."

Ettu changed the subject, perhaps guessing I didn't want to keep talking about Ishtar. I sat there for a few minutes, but I didn't know any of the people she and Merytre were talking about, so I went to bed. Marduk be damned, but I wouldn't let Ishtar find me waiting up for her. I knew I wouldn't sleep, though, with my mind whirling with thoughts of what exactly was happening between her and Pharaoh.

I heard Ettu and Merytre go off to bed not long after I did and a bird outside my window had begun its pre-dawn song before Ishtar returned. Her footsteps paused at the door to my bedchamber, as if debating whether to come in. I closed my eyes, feigning sleep, and she went on to her own chamber.

I finally dozed off, although it felt like I had barely fallen asleep before the bird at my window was joined by others, their songs too loud to sleep through. I could hear someone walking around the sitting chamber, but there were no voices to tell me who it was. It wouldn't be Ishtar, though. Not after she had returned so late.

It was Ahmose who was already up.

"Well?" she asked.

I sighed, searching for a way to frame the evening as more pleasant than it was, but before I could speak, Ettu came up behind me.

"Pharaoh was his usual self, from all accounts," she said. "My lady, I have laid out a gown for you to wear today."

Her attempt at changing the subject didn't dissuade Ahmose.

"What is his usual self?" she asked. "Is this a good thing or bad?"

Ettu pitched her voice low, probably so it wouldn't carry to Ishtar, although I doubted my sister was awake. Not if she had spent the whole night being plied with wine by Pharaoh.

"He ignored Lady Kassaya in favour of Ishtar," Ettu said.

Ahmose gave me a thoughtful look.

"I see," she said. "And how does my lady feel about this?"

"She is offended, of course," Ettu said, before I could reply. "She is the Ornament, after all. Ishtar is merely a servant, just like you and me."

Ahmose raised her eyebrows, indicating she still waited for my reply.

"Yes, I am offended," I said. "Although hardly surprised. But also…"

My voice trailed away and my cheeks heated. I was too embarrassed to reveal my lack of experience.

"Go on," Ahmose said.

"I am also a little relieved. That he didn't expect to bed me straight away. I don't know what happened after I left, but at least he didn't expect that from me."

"It would be your first time." If Ahmose was at all surprised, it didn't show in either her voice or her face.

"Yes, of course. Father wouldn't have sent me here otherwise."

"Do you know what would be expected of you?" she asked.

"Well, yes," I stammered. I thought I did, anyway, not that I would have admitted my uncertainty.

"If you need any advice, we can talk privately." Ahmose must have sensed my unwillingness to say more. "And there are other ways I can help you. Ways to make a man unable to perform, if that is your wish."

"Father sent me here to bear sons for Pharaoh," I said. "I hardly think he would…"

I didn't know how to finish, but Ahmose only nodded.

"Come to me if you need to," she said. "Whatever it is you need."

Merytre had slipped into the chamber while we were talking and soon a knock on the door signalled the arrival of my maids. Another day had begun. A day in which I had finally met Pharaoh, and in which he had met my sister.

CHAPTER 9

Ishtar didn't come stumbling from her chamber until well after noon. Her eyes were bloodshot and she already smothered a yawn.

"Good afternoon," I said evenly. I hadn't decided what to say about last night, so for now had resolved to pretend it hadn't happened. Ishtar had no such qualms.

"Oh, Sister," she said, dropping to her knees in front of me. "He was terribly rude to you."

From where I sat on the couch, her eyes were only a little below mine. I searched them for some sign of her true feelings, trying to convince myself her apparent remorse was real. I knew her better than that, though. I couldn't forget the hope I saw on her face when I said she would go with me. She had intended to use the situation to her advantage if she could.

"You will not accompany me again for any official event," I said.

She hung her head and seemed to wipe a tear from her eye. It was elegantly done, of course, and would have looked sincere to someone who didn't know her as well as I did.

"Forgive me, Sister," she said. "I didn't know what to do."

"Did he bed you?"

She sighed and didn't look at me.

"Answer me, Ishtar, and remember you stay here only because I allow it."

"Yes." Her voice was so soft I barely heard her.

I had expected to feel angry — any son she bore now should have been mine — but I felt only pity. This was the fate she had tried so hard to avoid, and yet it had found her anyway.

"Sister, I am sorry you are so displeased with me," she said. "I never meant for it to be like this."

"Oh, I know. You did your best to avoid being sent here at all. Don't think I have forgotten. What happened to him anyway? The man who got you with child? I cannot imagine Father allowed him to escape without punishment."

"I refused to give Father his name." For the first time since she had entered the chamber this morning, Ishtar looked me in the eyes. "I knew he would be exiled at least. Maybe worse. But he didn't do anything wrong. I let him think I loved him. That if I was with child, I would petition Father to let us marry."

"He didn't know Father had already promised you to Pharaoh?"

"He did, but I told him Father couldn't send me away if I already carried a child. I convinced him it was our best chance to be together."

"So he was just as much a victim of your plan as I was." I didn't bother trying to keep the bitterness from my voice. "Did you even ask Father to let you marry him?"

Ishtar sat back on her heels and looked away for a few moments before she answered.

"Of course not," she said. "He was... not someone I could ever marry. But he was in love with me, or at least he was in love with the idea of me, and it was easier to be with someone who thought he loved me than if he was only using me to get nearer to Father."

"Did you not fear punishment yourself? You must have known Father would be angry."

"Oh, he was." She finally looked at me again. "Sister, I have never seen him so angry. After you left, he confined me to my chambers and said I wouldn't be allowed out until the babe was born. He didn't want anyone to see me like that, unwed and yet with child. I think he thought that if I disappeared, everyone would think I had gone to Egypt and nobody would ever know what had really happened."

"Surely he would have allowed you to leave your chamber once the child was born, though?"

"I don't know. I think he had some other plan for me. He never said what, though, and of course, the babe didn't live long enough to be born."

It was hard not to pity her, even though it was probably the first time in her life that Ishtar didn't get what she wanted.

"Sister, I have always regretted the way my actions impacted on you," she said. "I knew it would mean you had to be sent in my place, but I..."

"What?" I asked. "You decided your life was more important than mine?"

"No."

We looked at each other for a long moment.

"Yes," she said at last. "I knew you would be unhappy, but I thought you would change your mind. Once you got here and settled in."

"Well, I haven't changed my mind, and now we are both stuck here, so your plan didn't work very well."

She blinked at me tearfully and, despite my sympathy, I couldn't bear to look at her. She was so good at feigning remorse.

"Leave me," I said. "I don't want to see your face again today."

She fled. The chamber was silent for a few moments, although I could almost feel how hard Ettu was thinking. I sighed and slumped back against the couch.

"I didn't handle that very well, did I?" I said when nobody commented.

"It is difficult," Ettu said. "For myself, I was to be sent regardless of which sister came, but I understand your anger."

"You think it misplaced, though?" There was something about Ettu's voice that said she didn't agree, even if she understood.

"It is not my place to judge," she said.

"You usually feel free to share your opinions. Why stop now?"

"I think perhaps I'll go for a walk." Ettu got to her feet. "Merytre, would you accompany me?"

They left and then it was just Ahmose and me in the sitting chamber. I closed my eyes to avoid looking at her.

"What about you?" I asked. "Do you, too, think I am wrong?"

It took Ahmose a while to answer and I held my tongue while I waited. I would at least try not to offend this last of my companions.

"I think there are no good answers," she said finally. "In a situation such as this, where there are two daughters and one must be sent to marry a foreign king, but neither wants to go.

However, as you said, you are both here now. It seems to me it would be better for you to direct your anger towards your father. If he hadn't agreed to send a daughter, neither you nor your sister would be here now."

"Neither would you."

"There is that, and I admit I'd rather be here, no matter the circumstances, than in Babylon."

Although a defence of my homeland wanted to burst out of me, I swallowed it down. There was no point arguing with Ahmose over which country was best. We each had our reasons for preferring the country of our birth and I supposed neither of us was wrong.

Just as maybe Ishtar wasn't wrong to prefer to stay in Babylon. Yes, she was selfish to act as she did, but could I be sure I would have done anything different if I was in her position? Would I have willingly left Babylon and travelled to a foreign land where the people were strangers to me? Would I have given up everything I knew if I could see a way out of it? I wasn't sure I knew the answer to that.

CHAPTER 10

*E*ttu and Merytre returned an hour or so later. Ettu shot me an assessing look, as if wondering whether I was in a better mood.

"I'm sorry," I said. "I was unfair."

She came to sit beside me.

"I know you are angry," she said. "But I can't help thinking there must be a way we can use this to our advantage."

"How? Pharaoh saw both of us and he chose her."

"Are you really that disappointed?" Her voice was hesitant, as if she was still trying to gauge my mood. "You were disillusioned after his speech the other day. I can't imagine you actually wanted him to pay you that sort of attention."

I started to reply, but stopped to examine my feelings first. I suspected what I had been about to say wasn't really the truth. After the way I had already treated Ettu today, I didn't want to lie to her as well.

"No, I suppose not," I said. "I think I am more offended than anything. That once again it is Ishtar who is seen as the special one. Just once I'd like someone to see me as special."

It was more than I meant to say and I closed my mouth firmly before anything else came out.

"Perhaps if he is besotted with her," Ahmose said slowly, as if still unravelling her thoughts. "We could use that to have her gain something from him. Information, maybe. Or some special favour for you."

"Yes," Ettu said. "There will be a way we can make use of this. We should think carefully, though. This is not the time to be hasty. You might only have one opportunity to use Ishtar and you don't want to waste it."

"In the meantime," Merytre said, "maybe you should speak with her. She looked like she felt terrible about what happened."

I wanted to say Ishtar never felt bad about anything she did, but I restrained myself. It would sound petty and childish, even if it was my honest opinion. Her contrition was a pretence, designed to elicit my sympathy so I wouldn't send her away. Not that I really would. Or, at least, I didn't think I would. She was my sister after all, and she had no means with which to support herself if I turned her out. Father had sent her to me and it was my obligation to look after her. Whether I wanted it or not.

My best option was to do as they suggested and look for a way to use Ishtar to my advantage. She had certainly not hesitated to use me. I had only been thinking about how Ishtar had ruined my chance for Pharaoh to notice me, at least in the short term, and about how she would likely give him a son long before I ever did.

But perhaps she could use her influence with him to introduce me again. Given his immediate fascination with her, he probably wouldn't even remember me. There was no need to remind him we had met before. Ishtar could merely introduce her sister and I would have another chance. I could still fulfil my duty to my father and to Babylon, despite Ishtar's presence.

"Are you going to sit with Lady Tiye this morning?" Ettu asked. "The distraction might be good for you."

"Yes, I think I will," I said.

Once again it was Nammu who opened Tiye's door when I knocked. She admitted me without even the smallest sneer, then disappeared into another chamber. I guessed Tiye must have impressed on her the precariousness of her position. Tiye lounged on a couch, dressed, as always, as if she was about to meet with Pharaoh. Her pleated skirt and lacy sleeves were far more elaborate than the simple shift I wore last night.

"Well," she said. "I hear your sister made quite the impression."

"How did you hear about that already?"

"I have my ways."

She arched her eyebrows at me and clearly didn't intend to reveal her source. It had to be either one of the nearly naked serving women or a guard. She surely couldn't have seen Pharaoh already in the hours since Ishtar had left him. I sat opposite her with a sigh.

"It troubles you, it would seem," she observed.

"Humiliates me, more like."

If Tiye thought I was taking the situation hard, perhaps she would be a little freer with her comments. I might learn something useful.

"He has always liked a beautiful woman," Tiye said. "You must have noticed the women who attend to him while he dines."

"It would be hard to miss them," I said. "I didn't quite know where to look."

To my surprise, Tiye laughed.

"We Egyptians take little issue with nudity," she said. "Other peoples are not so free with it."

"Where I come from, we would never have naked women to serve us at dinner."

"I'm sure they weren't naked."

"They might as well have been."

The girdles around their waists did nothing to hide their bodies.

"The thing you need to understand about Pharaoh is that he likes to look at beauty." Tiye straightened a couple of pleats in her skirt, as if to draw my attention to her fine gown. "And he likes women. Lots of them."

"One only has to look around to see that. I never realised one man could have so many wives."

"And yet he has only one queen." Tiye's voice was bitterer than I had heard from her before, making me wonder whether she had inadvertently revealed something true about herself to me.

"Is that a position you would want for yourself?" I asked.

"Of course. Wouldn't any woman?" She looked me right in the eyes.

"Not me. I never wanted any of this."

"And now your sister is here."

"Does everyone already know?"

She shrugged. "Not everyone, I suppose."

I leaned back against the couch, but quickly sat up again as I realised how inelegant that would look next to Tiye, who held herself so gracefully, even lounging as she was.

"I have never been so surprised as when Ishtar walked into my chambers," I said.

"Why is she here?"

"Your spies haven't told you?"

She gave me something that might have been either a smile or a grimace.

"No information leaves your chambers, not now Nammu has left your service at any rate. Your lady's maids are either unusually discreet or completely ignorant of whatever happens in there."

I hesitated. Should I tell her the truth or give her a story that might preserve Ishtar's reputation? I decided to repeat only what Ishtar had already told Pharaoh.

"Our father sent her to serve me," I said. "He thought she would learn humility."

"I see."

Tiye contained her reactions well and I couldn't tell whether she knew it wasn't the full truth. I needed to change the subject before I told her more than I meant to.

"Do you have any children?" It was the first thing that came into my mind.

"Six of them," she said. "All sons of Pharaoh."

"Do they live here?" I hadn't noticed any evidence of children in her chambers.

"Of course not." She gave me a look that said it was a foolish question. "They live in Pharaoh's palace. He keeps most of his sons close to him."

"Most?"

"The oldest, Ramses, lives in Memphis. He is heir, for now at least. But my son, Pentaweret, is the second oldest of Pharaoh's living sons. If Ramses were to go to the West, Pentaweret would be heir."

"Would you become queen then?"

She frowned at me.

"Of course not," she said. "Not as long as Isis still lives and Pharaoh still wants her. But that is a matter for the gods. We mortals have no knowledge of their plans."

It surprised me she wasn't scheming to become queen. Or perhaps she was but didn't trust me enough to tell me.

"Have you heard anything about Nebtu?" I asked to change the subject.

"No." Tiye frowned. "As much as we Ornaments are competitors, I don't like to see a woman go missing."

"Do you have any idea what has happened to her?"

She only looked at me and didn't answer. So, she knew more than she was saying. Tiye, it seemed, was a woman who would simply not answer rather than tell a lie. That would likely be a useful thing to understand about her.

"You must know something." Perhaps an appeal to her ego would loosen her tongue. "If anyone here has uncovered information about her, it would be you."

Tiye looked down at her hands, breaking our eye contact, and shook her head a little. Her response confused me. She almost looked… afraid.

"Tiye, are you well?" I asked before I could change my mind.

She gave a heavy sigh.

"You should be careful," she said. "Keep your servants close to you. None of you should be alone. As you have seen, women here go missing."

CHAPTER 11

 I mused over Tiye's strange reaction as I returned to my chambers. Her words had left me uneasy and I was grateful it was only a short walk. Few folk had reason to come to this hallway that led only to her and my chambers. It would be easy for a woman to disappear from here. Ettu was waiting outside the door when I arrived.

"What are you doing out here?" My discomfort left my tone sharper than I intended and she gave me a puzzled look. "You shouldn't be out here alone."

"I have heard nothing that suggests it is improper for a woman in my position to be alone in the hallway."

"I didn't say it was improper."

"You're thinking about Lady Nebtu?" she asked.

"Someone within the Palace was involved. Probably several someones. There's no other way she could leave the grounds."

"Maybe she didn't. Maybe she's still here."

"Locked in a chamber somewhere?"

Ettu shrugged. "Has anyone actually searched the Palace?

Done a proper search, I mean? Every chamber, all through the gardens and the buildings behind the Palace. The stables, the chapel."

"I don't know."

We eyed each other.

"The administrators might have locked her up like they did to both you and me," she said. "We could put together a search team. There must be plenty of women worried about her who would help us look."

"I don't know enough people here to organise such a thing."

"Lady Tiye does."

I couldn't ask Tiye. Not when it was clear she was keeping some secret about Nebtu's disappearance. I told Ettu about Tiye's strangeness when I asked if she knew what had happened, and she frowned.

"Is there any possibility she might be involved?" she asked. "Removing competition? We know she has done it before."

"I don't think so. She seemed… maybe not worried, but certainly disturbed. And she warned me to be careful. Surely she wouldn't do that if she was involved herself. But anyway, why are you out here? You were supposed to be resting."

"I wanted to tell you something privately. Before you walk in there and find out." She walked down the hallway a little way, out of earshot of anyone who might be just on the other side of the door, and I followed. "Pharaoh has sent for Ishtar. She is to go to his palace tonight."

"His palace? He isn't coming here?"

"It is almost unheard of, from what I understand," Ettu said. "Especially for a woman who is not an Ornament."

"Ettu, do you think she will be safe?" I set one hand to my chest, feeling how hard my heart beat. As angry as I was with

Ishtar — for many reasons — she was still my sister. "We know women have gone missing from both palaces. Maybe someone should go with her."

"I doubt she will be sent without an escort, and he is sending transport for her."

"I agree there's no way the administrators would allow an Ornament to travel to Pharaoh's palace unescorted, but a maid? Even one summoned by Pharaoh?"

"But neither will they allow anyone else to go with her," Ettu said. "Certainly not you, and I doubt they would let me or Merytre go."

"One of us could use Ahmose's potion. We could follow Ishtar and keep an eye on her."

"She will likely be taken to a private chamber," she said, shaking her head. "Even with Ahmose's potion, we won't get in. Not unless she also has a potion to let us walk through closed doors. There won't be much reason for the guards to open the door again once both Ishtar and Pharaoh are inside."

"And I suppose there is just as much danger to whoever follows her as to Ishtar herself. Probably more so since we would be alone the whole time."

"Have you considered..." Her voice trailed off and she looked away down the hallway as if she couldn't bear to meet my eyes.

"Say it," I said. "Whatever it is."

"Have you considered that Pharaoh might make her an Ornament? I know that wasn't your father's intention in sending her, but surely he has no control over the situation, not now she is here."

Or was that his intention all along? Did he send me for the sake of being seen to uphold the alliance, with a plan to send Ishtar to follow me? The loss of her babe might simply have given him reason to send her earlier than he had intended. Maybe he meant to take the babe from her once it was born and send Ishtar to Egypt anyway. He could have hired a wet nurse and had the child raised in the palace. The babe was his grandchild, after all. Ishtar said she thought he still had some plan for her.

"By the way," Ettu said, before I could figure out how to reply. "I have the letter from Lady Henutmire for Lady Nebtu's family."

And I had been about to suggest none of us should go out alone for a while, at least not until we knew what had happened to Nebtu. But I'd already told Henutmire I could get her letter out.

"I can take it tomorrow," Ettu said. "If I can get it to Half, he will be able to arrange for it to be sent to Lady Nebtu's family. And it will give me a chance to find out what folk are saying about Ishtar after tonight's visit."

Would I be risking Ettu's life if I sent her out alone? It might give us valuable information, not least about whether there was any danger to Ishtar in Pharaoh's palace. Could I afford not to send Ettu, no matter the risk?

"Do it," I said, and hoped Ettu would never realise I had put Ishtar's life above hers.

CHAPTER 12

$\mathcal{B}$y late afternoon, Ishtar still hadn't returned to my chambers. I sent Ettu and Merytre to find her, with strict instructions to stay together at all times. Ahmose and I waited together in the sitting chamber. I wasn't sure an old woman like her would be much deterrent if someone came to drag me away, but none of us were alone, and that seemed the best I could do right now.

I had chewed all the nails off one hand before I realised what I was doing. I tucked my hands beneath my thighs to stop myself from chewing the rest. My maids would be horrified at the state of my nails and I was sure I'd have to listen to many comments about it while they remedied my sorry appearance.

Ettu and Merytre returned with Ishtar, who looked unusually reticent. She came in but remained by the door, her gaze fixed on the floor. I ignored her, determined it wouldn't be me who spoke first. After a couple of piteous sighs from her, my resolution crumbled.

"I assume you have heard Pharaoh has summoned you?" My tone was only a little frostier than I meant it to be.

"Sister, I am sorry," she said, looking at me from beneath her lashes. It was the face she used when our father was angry with her and she was pretending to be repentant even as she worked to get what she wanted from him. It was always effective with Father, but she forgot how well I knew her. "I won't go if it displeases you."

"You can't refuse Pharaoh's summons. Given you are supposed to be my servant, there would likely be consequences for me as well as for you."

"Are you terribly mad at me?" She crossed the room to kneel at my feet. "I can't bear to know you are angry with me."

"The possibility didn't seem to bother you last night." It was cruel of me and I knew it even as the words came out of my mouth. I sighed and tried to reign in my irritation. "You should go prepare yourself. You do not want to keep him waiting."

"Would one of your maids help me dress?" She gave me a sly look from beneath her lashes. "I fear I wouldn't know what was appropriate to wear."

"Go."

She left, although not without a heavy sigh as if to ensure everyone knew how badly she was being treated. If I hadn't known her my whole life, I might have believed her apology, but she wasn't sorry she had attracted Pharaoh's attention. What woman would be, in her position? The only reason Ishtar was sorry was because she feared I might turn her out.

"Should I…" Ettu's voice trailed away.

"Yes," I said. "Go help her. I won't dishonour our father by letting her present herself to Pharaoh looking any less than she should."

Merytre looked at me enquiringly and I nodded. They both disappeared down the hallway and once again, it was just Ahmose and me left in the sitting chamber.

"It is a fine situation she has gotten herself into." Ahmose's mild tone made the words seem more like an observation than a judgement.

I sighed.

"That's Ishtar," I said. "She always has to be the centre of attention. I should have expected he would notice her. I was a fool to take her with me."

"There are things a woman can do if she wants a man to notice her."

"Like what?" I leaned back against the couch and closed my eyes. When Ahmose didn't reply, I opened my eyes to check why. She just sat there, looking at me and waiting for me to understand the significance of her words.

"Oh," I said as I realised. "A spell?"

"There are spells for many things," she said. "One might seek to attract a man's attention or to make him lose interest in another."

"So I could…" My voice trailed away.

I couldn't do that to Ishtar. Could I? Although she had won Pharaoh's attention on a night when his focus should have been on me, she had done it fairly by using nothing more than her looks. Would it be unfair for me to use a spell to reverse such an attraction? Or to elevate myself?

"I don't know," I said. "I'm not sure I want to do something like that."

"The other option is to let this situation with your sister play out and see what happens. He may lose interest soon enough, and then you can put yourself forward again."

Ishtar might already be carrying his son by then. How much more would that advance her in his interest? Could I even compete with her after that?

"I will think about it," I said. "I can promise no more than that."

"What of your plan?" Ahmose asked. "That Tall and Half would come here if they needed to flee? What will you do now Ishtar is using the chamber you had intended for them?"

"I suppose someone will have to share," I said. "If Tall and Half need somewhere to go, I won't turn them away. We will manage. There is enough room, or perhaps I will tell Panouk I need bigger chambers and see what happens."

Someone knocked and Merytre came to let in the servants with our evening meal. I watched from my position on the couch as they brought in tray after tray, setting it down on various tables. An appetising aroma made my stomach grumble and I realised I hadn't eaten since breakfast.

"Well, I, for one, don't intend to let this go cold," I said, getting to my feet. "Get yourself some dinner, Ahmose."

But before either of us could do so, Ishtar returned, followed by Ettu and Merytre. As angry as I still was with her, I couldn't help seeing how beautiful they had made her. She wore a silvery gown made of linen so fine it was almost transparent and which did little to hide her shapely curves. I supposed it was one that had been arranged for me, although nobody had yet suggested I wear it.

"She can't wear that," I said. "It's indecent."

"That's what I thought," Ettu said. "But Merytre assures us such a gown is perfectly acceptable here."

"It is true," Merytre said. "Look how fine the linen is. Only the very finest of fabrics are so sheer."

Indeed, Ishtar wore more than the servant women who attended Pharaoh.

"But it covers nothing," I said. "Ishtar, you can't possibly wear that. Father would be shocked."

"Father isn't here," Ishtar said, and the look on her face made me suspect she had chosen the gown herself. "But if it displeases you, I won't wear it. I am sure they can find me something else."

I shot Ettu a look, thinking she would agree with me, but she shrugged.

"If Merytre says it is appropriate, we should trust her," she said. "I'm sure I can't see how it can be considered decent, but there's much we don't understand about the people here."

"Tiye said the Egyptians aren't very bothered about nudity," I said.

Ishtar did look exquisite. They had arranged her hair in the style that seemed to be most popular, the one Merytre favoured, with one section swept forward and pinned up, and the rest falling loose over her shoulders.

"They haven't shaved your hair yet," I said to her.

Ishtar raised one hand to stroke her long locks.

"They wanted to, but I refused," she said.

"I tried to refuse too. But they shaved me anyway."

"I am sorry, Sister. Do you wish for me to go shave my head right now?"

I sighed. Only Ishtar could make such a thing sound like a sacrifice for my benefit. If I said yes, though, she would find some reason not to do it and still manage to make it sound like it was all for me.

"No, you should leave or you will be late," I said. "You don't want to keep Pharaoh waiting."

"Merytre and I will see her to the gates," Ettu said.

The three of them left. Ishtar gave me a beseeching look on her way out the door, as if waiting for me to offer some kind of blessing on her evening with Pharaoh, or at least to say I wasn't angry he had chosen her instead of me. I looked away and pretended I hadn't noticed.

CHAPTER 13

It was well after dawn before Ishtar returned this time. We had all risen by then and the four of us were waiting in the sitting chamber when she finally slipped in. Relief surged within me. After all our talk about missing women, I had slept only briefly, and my unease had grown the longer she was gone. Ishtar's hair was in disarray and it covered her face as she closed the door behind her.

My mind whirled and I couldn't think of a greeting that didn't sound sarcastic. It was Ishtar who spoke.

"I am going to bed," she whispered and fled down the hallway.

"She seems…" Merytre's voice trailed away.

"Upset," Ettu said. "I thought so too."

She's just spent her second night with the most powerful man in the country, I thought. What does she have to be upset about? I didn't let the words pass my lips. They sounded jealous and nasty, and as bitter as I felt, I was also trying to remember Ishtar was my sister and that she, like me, was a stranger in a foreign land. Perhaps she made her way here in the only way she knew how: using her looks. Where I relied on my wits, Ishtar had always used her beauty to get what she wanted.

"Are you going to visit with Lady Tiye today?" Ettu asked me.

"Yes, I still need to maintain the facade of cleaning her bathing chamber."

"Ask what she has heard about Ishtar," she said.

"I will, but first I'm going to eat in the dining chamber."

As Ettu and I emerged into the hallway, we came face to face with Amankhau.

"Aah, Lady Kassaya," he said, giving me a smile that made my insides roll. "I have the confirmation you requested."

"Confirmation?" It was the first time we had spoken since he locked me in a chamber and threatened to haul me before a magistrate, and I couldn't think what he could possibly mean.

"Panouk said you wanted to hear from the messenger who went to Lady Nebtu's father. Step forward, lad."

From behind him, a boy of around ten years old appeared.

"Go on then," Amankhau said, poking his shoulder. "Deliver your message."

"The Lady Nebtu's father confirms she has safely returned to his house," the boy said.

I had almost forgotten Panouk agreed to send a messenger to Nebtu's family. I had been so sure she didn't go home that I had dismissed the conversation from my mind.

"Are you sure?" I asked the boy. It was a daft question, but it came out of my mouth without thought.

He shot a look up at Amankhau, as if seeking permission to answer.

"Of course he is sure," Amankhau said in a hearty voice. "Now, let's agree this matter is resolved, shall we? You asked for confirmation from Lady Nebtu's father and there you have it. The messenger confirms she has returned home."

"I see."

I left him standing there with the boy and continued down the hallway. Beside me, Ettu was silent and when I glanced at her, I found she was frowning.

"Did that seem odd to you?" I asked once we were out of Amankhau's earshot. "I can't quite figure it out, but something isn't right."

"The messenger was awfully young to have travelled all the way to Lady Nebtu's family and back," Ettu said. "I heard they live in Behdet, which apparently is not all that far from Thebes, but still, I am surprised a boy was sent, rather than a grown man."

"I suppose Panouk wanted to ensure the messenger could report directly to me since that was what I asked. He couldn't have brought a man into the palace."

"He could have had you go to the gates to hear the message. Or he could have sent one of the modified men. Marduk knows there seems to be an abundance of them around here."

"It was the way the boy spoke," I said. "That was what bothered me. It was as if they were words he had memorised."

"And when you asked if he was sure, he didn't know how to reply."

"Because that wasn't part of the message he memorised. It wasn't part of what the administrators told him to say."

"The messenger was a fake." Ettu quickened her stride as if eager to put more distance between Amankhau and us. I hurried to keep up with her.

"I agree," I said. "And that only convinces me more than ever that something happened to Nebtu."

"I suppose Lady Henutmire's letter warns Lady Nebtu's family not to risk replying to her. So we will not know if her letter contradicts what the administrators have told them."

"Speaking of Henutmire," I said as we turned down the final hallway and I spotted her approaching from the opposite end. We met in front of the doors to the dining chamber.

"Greetings, Kassaya," she said. "I trust you are well?"

"I am." I glanced around to make sure nobody could overhear and lowered my voice. "It will be done tonight," I whispered.

Henutmire's eyes widened slightly. So, she hadn't thought I could actually get a message out.

"Very good," she murmured.

We made our way to our usual tables and Ettu fussed with my skirt before she took her place against the wall. Henutmire's maid, a young girl whose skin was too dark for her to be Egyptian, went to stand beside her. From the corner of my eye, I saw them exchange a few comments. I hoped that meant Ettu was making allies of her own here.

The servants brought trays of food and drinks, and for a while, I was busy making selections. At last, my table was full and I was able to wave them away.

"I saw Amankhau on my way here," I said.

"Always a pleasant way to start the day," Henutmire said and I found myself grinning at the sarcasm in her words. "Although normally we only have the pleasure of seeing him at night. Panouk is usually the one in charge during the day."

It was nice to know it wasn't just me who despised Amankhau. I drizzled honey over my bread and took a bite. It was chewy, still warm from the oven, and the sweetness of the honey made my mouth water.

"He had a messenger with him," I said when I could speak

again. "A boy of maybe ten years who claimed to bear a message from Nebtu's father."

"Really?" Henutmire gave me a cautious look. "Why would Amankhau take such a message to you? I thought you hardly knew her."

"When I asked Panouk about Nebtu, he insisted she had returned to her father. I asked him to send a messenger to seek confirmation. I suppose he told Amankhau to look after it. Anyway, the boy said her father confirmed she had arrived there."

Henutmire chewed her bread, a thoughtful look on her face.

"About ten years, you said?" she asked, her voice low.

"More or less."

"A very young messenger."

"I thought that too."

She gave me a look that seemed filled with significance.

"I suppose we have our confirmation then," she said, rather loudly. "The messenger confirmed Nebtu returned to her father's home. There is no cause for us to be concerned."

I was certain that wasn't what she believed. The words didn't ring true and she had been worried enough to risk being involved with smuggling an illicit letter out of the Palace. Perhaps she thought someone might be listening. Maybe spying for the administrators, or even for Pharaoh.

"I agree," I said. "I feel greatly relieved at knowing she is safe."

Ineni arrived and claimed the table on the other side of Henutmire.

"Greetings," she said to us both.

I murmured a reply, suddenly feeling a little shy. I had spoken to Ineni only once, that first morning I dined here. I didn't know Henutmire much better, but something about her put me at ease right away.

"I am having a small gathering in my chamber tomorrow night," Ineni said. She seemed to direct her words to Henutmire, so I busied myself with my meal. "You should come. Both of you."

I was so surprised at being included in her invitation that I didn't immediately reply.

"Be warned, Kassaya," Henutmire said. "Ineni might say it's a small gathering, but she doesn't mean there will be a small amount of wine. I still remember the way my head ached after the last of Ineni's *small gatherings*."

"Thank you," I said. "I will look forward to it."

"Don't eat before you come," Ineni said. "There will be plenty of food. And there is no need to bring a maid. It is just a small gathering, as I said, and we like to be able to speak freely without any servants listening."

I nodded and quickly filled my mouth with bread so she wouldn't expect a reply. Surely I would be safe with other Ornaments. I could have Ettu and Merytre walk me there, and they could return in a couple of hours to collect me. Ishtar and Ahmose could wait together in my chambers and none of us would be wandering the hallways alone. We would all be safe in company.

CHAPTER 14

I went to sit with Tiye, but she seemed distracted and I didn't stay long. If she had heard anything else about Ishtar, she didn't volunteer it and I couldn't find the right words to ask. Ettu was waiting for me at the end of the hallway.

"Why didn't you go back to my chambers?" I asked.

"What is the difference between me standing in Lady Tiye's hallway or making my way alone through the Palace? Surely I am safer here, where you would hear me scream, than wandering the hallways alone."

"I suppose you are right. I hate this, though. Always having to think about whether we are safe. We shouldn't have to worry about such a thing in a place like this."

"It is as it is," she said with a shrug. "If we could figure out what happened to Lady Nebtu, maybe we would realise we don't have to worry so much. But for now, I agree we should be cautious."

"Let's go for a walk. I haven't been outside for days and I'm longing for some fresh air."

We made our way out to the gardens and roamed along the pathways for a while. I had spent little time outside since we arrived. I should make an effort to get out every day, at least for a few minutes. The grounds were gorgeous and immaculately maintained, and it was a shame to not spend time out here to appreciate them.

"I think I had forgotten how beautiful it is here," Ettu said. "I have been so caught up in what has been happening — Lady Nebtu, Ishtar, the matter with Lady Tiye's jewels — that I have barely even looked out a window."

"That reminds me," I said. "I never asked what happened after Amankhau took me away. He said you confessed to having stolen Tiye's finger ring."

Ettu took a long time to answer and I was beginning to regret having asked. Perhaps she was still too upset about it. I should have waited until she offered to tell me.

"He threatened to beat me if I didn't confess," she said at last. "Then he said you had confessed on my behalf and that would be sufficient testimony for the magistrate. When I still wouldn't say what he wanted me to, he said he wasn't going to bother the magistrate but would have both you and me sent to the slave mines in Nubia. He said we would be forced to dig for gold through all the daylight hours for the rest of our lives."

"So you gave him a confession?" I could hardly blame her. The slave mines sounded like a terrible fate.

"I said what he told me to." Her voice was low. "He promised that if I confessed, I would get my chance at a trial. I hoped..."

"What?" I prompted.

"I hoped that if there was a trial, you might speak on my behalf. I wasn't sure you would, but it was my only chance."

"Of course I would have. I had already decided it."

"But then, of course, you bargained for my freedom and there was no need for a trial." Ettu's voice was lighter now. "I'm not sure I ever thanked you properly."

I waved her away.

"There is no need," I said. "I would never let a servant of mine be punished for something she didn't do."

I spotted a figure some distance ahead of us, but it was only as we drew closer that I realised it was Gilukhipa, the Ornament from Mitanni. A maid followed a little way behind her. Gilukhipa raised her hand and gave me a smile that looked genuinely warm. I was surprised at her greeting. The last time I saw her — shortly after the incident with the jewels — she had only frowned at me. Maybe Tiye had told her I didn't really steal them.

"Kassaya," she said as we came within speaking distance. "I walk at this time every morning and haven't seen you here before."

"Ettu and I were just saying we have barely been outside since we arrived," I said. "There never seems to be enough time to walk around the gardens."

"You should make time." As Gilukhipa reached us, she turned to walk back in the direction I was headed, while Ettu dropped back to walk with her maid. "Everything else you must do will wait, but morning only comes once a day and it is truly the best time to appreciate the gardens. Unless you are the type who favours wandering the grounds at night."

My cheeks heated and I hoped she wouldn't notice. I hadn't seen Khaemmalu again since the night I arrived, but I was still embarrassed at the possibility he might have thought I was flirting with him. Gilukhipa's next words confirmed she had indeed noticed and had assumed the reason for my blush.

"Of course," she said. "If you are inclined to some secret tryst, night is a much better time for it. There are many private places in the grounds which are quite hidden in the dark."

"Oh," I stammered. "I wouldn't— I haven't—"

Gilukhipa laughed.

"You wouldn't be the first to have an affair with one of the guards, you know," she said, her voice lowered conspiratorially. "Or even with another Ornament, if that is more to your taste. But thank the gods they at least allow unmodified men to patrol the grounds. I think I would positively die of boredom otherwise."

My cheeks flamed and I knew they must be an unmissable shade of scarlet by now. She glanced at me and laughed even harder.

"Oh my," she said. "Maybe I am mistaken. You don't seem the type to have an affair."

"My father sent me to Pharaoh," I said. "He would be furious if…"

If I did what Ishtar did and got myself with child to a man who wasn't Pharaoh. Of course, it might well be Ishtar who bore Pharaoh's son, long before he ever bedded me.

"At least you know you have options," Gilukhipa said with a merry laugh.

"Are not affairs frowned on? I thought the point of allowing only modified men into the Palace was to ensure such things didn't happen."

"Oh, they are very frowned on. Illegal. He would certainly be executed if caught, and probably you as well. But the danger makes it that much sweeter, you see?"

"Executed?" I glanced at her, wondering whether I had misunderstood the Egyptian word she used.

"As an Ornament, you are Pharaoh's property. No other man may touch you."

Sutem had said something like that the day he helped me climb down from Tiye's window.

"Surely it is not worth the risk," I said.

She shrugged. "I suppose it depends."

"On what?"

"On how sweet the temptation is. And how bored you are."

Intent on our conversation, I wasn't paying attention to where I walked and I stumbled as my sandal caught on the edge of the path. My cheeks — still hot from thoughts of Khaemmalu — flamed again.

"I don't think I'll ever be bored enough to risk execution," I said.

"You might change your mind once you've been here a few years. This place is monotonous. When the banquets and the gossip and the walks through the gardens are finished, what else is there to do?"

"I suppose I have been filling my time well enough." With intrigue and plotting how to get messages out of the Palace.

Gilukhipa gave me a sideways look.

"I think there is more to you than it seems," she said. "But tell me. You have a new lady's maid and some say she is your sister. Is that true?"

"It is. Her name is Ishtar."

"I haven't seen her myself, but I have heard she is very beautiful. That anyone who saw the two of you together would know immediately you were sisters."

"We don't look all that much alike." My cheeks flamed at the compliment.

"I have heard otherwise."

She seemed to imply I was beautiful, but my looks were

nothing compared to Ishtar's. We walked in silence for a few moments while I tried to sort through my thoughts.

"I heard something else about your sister." Gilukhipa's tone was sly now.

"Oh?"

"I heard she made quite an impression on Pharaoh. That she has already spent a night with him."

So word hadn't yet gone out about him summoning her to his palace.

"Two nights, in fact," Gilukhipa continued.

I sighed in dismay. "I didn't think anyone knew yet."

"So it is true," she said. "I heard she went out last night and there was speculation the palanquin transporting her was Pharaoh's own. But nobody has been able to confirm it."

"And I just did."

If I had been more cautious with my words, I might have kept it secret a little longer. Although I couldn't have said why that seemed important. Everyone already knew about Pharaoh's immediate fascination with her.

"Are you going to Ineni's gathering tomorrow night?" she asked.

Gilukhipa's abrupt change of topic briefly disconcerted me. I hadn't expected her to be willing to leave the subject of Ishtar until she had wrung every drop of information she thought she might get from me.

"It would be rather awkward right now if she hadn't asked me," I said.

"I knew she would. We talked about who she was inviting. It's a rather select group."

"Are you close to her?"

Gilukhipa walked for a bit without replying. I wasn't sure whether she hadn't heard me or just didn't intend to answer, and was debating whether to ask again when she finally spoke.

"As close as you might get to anyone in this place," she said. "Make your alliances, Kassaya, but be careful who you share your secrets with. I must go now."

She turned and strode back the way we had come, moving swiftly along the path as if she wanted to put as much distance between us as possible. Her maid hurried after her.

Ettu caught up to me.

"Did you hear much of that?" I asked.

"Most of it. Her final comment was strange, don't you think?"

"Yes. I am not sure what to make of it."

"Perhaps it is no more than it seems. A friendly warning not to trust anyone until you are sure of them."

"Maybe," I said.

It had sounded like more than that, though, and Gilukhipa wasn't the first person here to warn me about not trusting anyone. I was starting to wonder what secrets the Palace of the Ornaments hid.

CHAPTER 15

 didn't see Ishtar again until late that afternoon. She hesitated in the doorway to the sitting chamber, as if wondering whether she was welcome to join us.

"Come and sit down, Ishtar," I said, striving for an even tone. I thought I almost managed it. As bitter as I was about how quickly she caught Pharaoh's attention, I needed to remember that she, like me, was a stranger in a foreign land. Father had sent her to me and I could hardly turn her out. We had to find a way to live together, and trying to make her feel like a servant wouldn't help. Ishtar was Ishtar. She was never going to change. She might pretend to be my maid for a while, but only so long as it suited her.

Ishtar sat on a couch that was a little away from anyone else and clasped her hands in her lap. She bowed her head and her loose hair fell down to shield her face.

"I have never seen you wear your hair like that before, Ishtar," Ettu said.

"Neither have I," I said.

Ishtar was always meticulous with her appearance. If she

had decided to leave her hair unbound, there was a reason for it. What was she hiding? I went to her and took her chin to raise her face. She flinched away from me.

"Ishtar, what is wrong?" I asked.

"Nothing."

Her voice was so soft, I could hardly hear her even though I stood right in front of her. She still clasped her hands, holding them so tightly that the ends of her fingers had turned white. Alarm bubbled up inside me. This was not just Ishtar playing for attention. Something was really wrong.

I sat beside her and tried to find the right words to encourage her to tell us whatever it was. Before I could figure out what to say, Ishtar sighed and pushed her hair back from her face. It was only then I saw the marks around her neck.

"What is that?" I raised my hand, meaning to move her hair so I could see it better.

"Don't touch it," she said quickly. "It is quite tender."

"Ishtar, how did that happen? Who did that to you?"

"Pharaoh was… rather rough with me last night."

She didn't look at me as she spoke.

"Pharaoh did that?" If anyone else in the chamber hadn't been able to hear her quiet words, they certainly heard me.

"Don't make a fuss," she said quickly. "Please."

"I'm not making a fuss. I'm just…" Shocked. Appalled. Horrified. "Why? Did you refuse him?"

He was a living god, after all. No doubt he had never been refused by a woman.

"No, he just—" She stopped and seemed to swallow hard. "That's what he likes."

"He likes to strangle you?"

"It's not like that. You wouldn't understand."

"No, Ishtar," I said. "I wouldn't. He never even looked at me when I met him."

A sob burst out of her and I regretted my hasty words.

"I'm sorry," I said. "That was cruel of me."

She ducked her head down so her hair covered her face.

"Ishtar, maybe you shouldn't go if he calls for you again."

"How can I not?" Her voice was small and even though I sat right beside her, I had to lean close to hear her. "He is a living god, as he likes to say. If he summons me, I cannot refuse."

"Surely we can report this." I looked to Merytre for confirmation. "What if we told Panouk?"

She gave Ishtar a pitying look and shook her head.

"I'm afraid not," she said. "Pharaoh is above any laws. There is nothing Panouk can do."

"What about the administrators at his palace? Or the police chief?"

"No." Ishtar's voice was stronger now and she brushed her hair back from her face so she could see me. "It would only make things worse. Please, Sister, promise me you will do nothing. Just forget you ever saw it."

I pressed my lips together, wanting to argue with her but knowing it would serve no purpose. I shook my head. It wasn't exactly an agreement, but she seemed satisfied enough.

CHAPTER 16

"Everyone in Pharaoh's palace is talking about her," Ettu announced when she returned shortly before dawn from seeing Tall and Half. As usual, I had slept on the couch to wait for her. "Half says everyone wants to know about the woman who is Pharaoh's latest obsession. They all think she is an Ornament. Some have figured out she is from Babylon and it was already known that a new Ornament had arrived, so of course they assume she is you."

I digested this news silently, trying to sort through my conflicted emotions. Resentment that Ishtar had upstaged me when she wasn't even supposed to be here. Annoyance the Ornaments were apparently so indistinguishable that one was easily mistaken for another. A tiny bit of satisfaction that it was a woman from my homeland who had gained Pharaoh's fascination, easily edged out by jealousy that Ishtar's arrival meant I didn't have a fair chance to get his attention myself.

"His queen, Lady Isis, is not happy," Ettu continued. "Half says she would never comment publicly, but apparently when she heard that Pharaoh intended to spend a second evening with Ishtar so soon, she berated him."

"How does Half know?" I asked.

"The servants talk," she said. "And for one such as Half, they don't even bother to stop when he passes. They don't think he has the wit to understand them, let alone tell anyone."

Her tone had turned bitter and I couldn't tell whether she was merely being protective of someone she considered a friend, or whether she felt more for him. It was none of my business, though. She would tell me if she wanted me to know, and until then I would pretend I noticed nothing.

"Did you give Half the message for Nebtu's family?" I asked instead.

"Yes, and he will take it to a courier as soon as he can."

"He is sure it is safe to do so?"

"There are no restrictions on messages leaving Pharaoh's palace," she reminded me. "And since Half can't read Egyptian, if the message did fall into the wrong hands, he could quite reasonably plead ignorance of the contents. It's just a letter someone asked him to see to a courier, and being new to the palace, he could say he didn't know who they were."

I swallowed down my mistrust. When did I become so accustomed to the ways of this place that it seemed dangerous for a servant to pass a letter to a courier? I wondered whether Henutmire had put her name to it. If it did go astray, could it be traced back to her?

"How is Tall?" I asked. "You haven't mentioned him yet."

"He said little while I was there," Ettu said. "Although he seemed concerned when Half and I were talking about Ishtar. I asked what he had heard to make him look so worried, but he wouldn't tell me."

"If folk are not cautious about what they say in front of Half, I'm sure they are even less cautious with Tall," I said. "He is probably learning much that could be useful to us."

"I will try again next time. I got the distinct feeling he knew something."

"I don't know why he wouldn't have told you." I rubbed my eyes. It was surely tiredness that made my thoughts feel so slow.

"It might be nothing more than malicious gossip." Ettu shrugged and didn't seem particularly concerned. "He knows Ishtar is your sister and he wouldn't want to pass on something hurtful."

I supposed that could be true, but I would rather know what he was worrying about, even if it was just gossip.

"Was there any other news?" I asked.

"Just that Half said to tell you if Pharaoh summons Ishtar for a third time, she should find a reason to decline. Pretend to be sick if she must. He was worried she is all anyone is talking about and that she will make an enemy of the queen if it continues."

"Ishtar is surely not the first woman Pharaoh has been enamoured with," I said with a shrug. "And Isis must know he has a whole palace of women he goes to."

"She does, and Half said that as long as the Ornaments are confined to their own palace, it seems the queen accepts the situation. But she is most unhappy about Pharaoh summoning Ishtar to the place where she herself lives."

"What could she do about it, though?" I asked. "I mean, it's not like she could tell Ishtar to leave."

A horrible thought occurred to me and from the look on Ettu's face, she must have thought the same.

"You don't think…" she whispered.

"Surely not."

Could the queen be responsible for the disappearing women?

"Have you heard anything about whether Nebtu was a current favourite of Pharaoh's?" I asked.

Ettu shook her head.

"I can try to find out," she said. "Although someone who would definitely know is Lady Tiye. I'm sure she pays close attention to who Pharaoh spends time with. But maybe you shouldn't visit with her in her chambers anymore. We don't know she isn't involved herself."

"Making a woman disappear in secret isn't Tiye's style." This was something I was certain of. "If she was going to act against another Ornament, she wouldn't try to hide it. And it's not only Nebtu. Other women have disappeared over the years. Merytre said she knew of fifteen, but that might not be all of them. Tiye even warned me not to be alone. She wouldn't do that if she was the one responsible."

"Of course, it's not just here either," Ettu said. "Women have disappeared from Pharaoh's palace as well. Don't forget the servant woman Half told me about."

"So it can't be Tiye. No matter what influence she has here, she surely couldn't arrange for a woman to disappear from there. Especially given there is no way for an Ornament to communicate with anyone outside the Palace."

"You already have a means of communication, and Lady Tiye has been here far longer. It's not unreasonable to think she has a way of passing messages between the two palaces."

"We can't go about assuming every woman we meet is responsible," I said.

Ettu gave me a look that said she didn't agree.

"Until we know what happened to Lady Nebtu and the

servant woman from Pharaoh's palace, I don't think we have any choice," she said. "Everyone is a suspect and we shouldn't trust anyone."

"I don't want to live like that. I have to believe there are people here we can trust. Good people."

"I'm sure that is the case, but right now, we don't know who they are."

"I think I can trust Tiye," I said. "Even if she knows more than she is saying. Until she gives me reason to think otherwise, I'm going to trust her."

CHAPTER 17

*B*y midafternoon, Ishtar still hadn't come out of her bedchamber, so I went to her. I knocked and heard a muffled sound that might have been an invitation. When I opened the door, Ishtar was sitting on the bed, looking unusually rumpled, as if she had been lying face down until just now. She didn't look up as I sat beside her. The red marks around her neck were turning purple.

"I'm sorry," I said. "I don't really know what else to say, but I am sorry."

"Not as sorry as me," she said studying her hands. "I have ruined both your life and my own, and look what it got me. I'm in exactly the position I was trying to avoid in the first place, except you are here too. If I have to be here, I'm grateful you are with me."

I pressed my lips together to stop myself from reminding her it was she who was here with me, not the other way around.

"Would you let Ahmose see your neck?" I asked instead. "It

looks like it is already bruising. She probably has something that will ease the pain."

Ishtar didn't look up from her hands.

"I shouldn't," she said. "Father told me quite firmly I was not to make a fuss or to draw attention to myself."

"How is allowing someone to treat an injury making a fuss? Besides, how would he even know?"

But she shook her head.

"It doesn't hurt that much," she said. "There is no need to bother Ahmose with such a thing."

I would let it go for now and try again later.

"Has Pharaoh told you when he wants to see you again?" I asked.

She inhaled shakily.

"No, and that makes it even worse," she said. "After he was finished" — she raised one trembling hand to her neck — "he only told me to go and that he would send for me when he wants me."

"We have some information from Half," I said. "You remember him?"

She made a sound that might have been an agreement. At least she didn't call him by his old nickname, which I had expected.

"He is worried about how much folk at Pharaoh's palace are talking about you. He said if Pharaoh calls for you again, you should find a reason to decline."

She made no answer, although I saw the way she clenched her hands together so tightly that her fingers went white.

"Perhaps you should try to rest," I said when she didn't reply.

I left her and went back out to the sitting chamber. Ettu,

Merytre and Ahmose were all relaxing in their favourite spots, looking much calmer than I felt.

"How is she?" Ahmose asked. "Can I do something for her?"

"I don't really know," I said. "I have never seen her like this before. Her neck is bruising. I suggested she should let you look at it, but she refused."

"She has had a terrible experience," Ahmose said. "Let her come to terms with it, then I'll see if she will accept an ointment to make the bruising fade faster."

"I didn't know you had medical knowledge." Merytre gave Ahmose an admiring look. "You know as much as a man might."

Ahmose scoffed. "Medical knowledge, no, but I do know herbs. Which ones will reduce swelling or draw the blood out when it pools beneath the skin. Herbs to calm nerves and reduce pain. All things that would be useful for Ishtar right now, if she will trust me."

Ishtar barely spoke to any of us over the next few days and I mostly let her be. Truth be told, I still struggled to reconcile my feelings about her. Anger festered inside me — the way she manipulated our father to have me sent in her place and how she so immediately drew Pharaoh's attention — and I was even more angry with myself for thinking such things after the abuse she had suffered. It was wrong of me to feel so much resentment towards her while she was injured and unhappy, but I didn't seem to be able to let go of my bitter thoughts.

Ettu was eager to visit Tall and Half again, and there were several pointed conversations between her and Ahmose about who should go next, before they agreed it would be Ettu. Once again, I spent the night on the couch to wait for her. I didn't bother trying to stay awake, knowing she would rouse me if I didn't hear her come in. But when I woke, the sun had risen and Ettu still hadn't returned. I was standing at the window, hoping to glimpse her coming through the grounds, when Merytre came in.

"Ettu's chamber is empty and her bed doesn't look like it was slept in," she said as she went to pour herself some melon juice. "Have you seen her?"

"She didn't come back," I said. "Maybe she was caught."

"More likely she ran out of time." She paused to take a long drink. "Ahmose says the potion only lasts twelve hours at most. If she was delayed, it might have worn off before she could get in the gates."

"And if she didn't realise in time, the guards would have seen her. They would know she shouldn't be out there and would want to know how she got out."

I turned back to the window, searching again for any sight of Ettu. Merytre came to stand beside me.

"Are you thinking she has been arrested?" she asked.

"I'm not sure it would be anything so formal. They might just lock her up until she tells them what they want to know. Last time, they threatened her with being beaten if she didn't confess."

And worse things. I didn't know whether Ettu had shared all the details with Merytre and it didn't feel like my place to tell her if she hadn't.

"They already think she is trouble, after that business with Lady Tiye's finger ring," Merytre said.

"I will go for a walk as soon as I am dressed," I said. "See if I can overhear anything from the guards about Ettu being caught. Or if she is still out there somewhere, maybe I will see her."

"How? The walls are far too high to see over. You will see nothing unless you happen to be standing in the right place as the gates open."

"I might at least hear something." I kept scanning the grounds, even though I knew I probably wouldn't see her from here. "You and Ahmose should go talk to some of the servants and see if they can tell you anything. Maybe you could even go up to the roof and see if you can spot her outside the gates."

"What would we say? We can't tell anyone Ettu went out and didn't come back."

"Maybe you could just ask what news there is today?" I suggested. "I don't want to make anyone more fearful than they already are after Nebtu's disappearance. If Ettu wasn't caught, we might yet be able to get her back inside without anyone knowing."

CHAPTER 18

By the time Ishtar finally emerged from her bedchamber, my lady's maids had arrived and were almost finished bathing and shaving me. My nose was already running from the aromatic oils they rubbed all over my skin.

Ishtar wore a double gown like an Egyptian woman. A pretty linen shawl around her shoulders was pulled high against her neck and pinned so it hid the bruises. It was the first time I had seen her in something other than her own Babylonian clothes, apart from that sheer obscenity she wore to see Pharaoh. Merytre or Ettu must have arranged new clothing for her. I wondered whether I should have thought to ask someone to do so earlier.

"Ugh, I can't stand these oils," I said to Ishtar. Maybe if I pretended everything was normal, she would do the same, and perhaps that would help her to feel better.

"I think they smell lovely," she said. "Everyone here is so fragrant."

"I could do with a little less fragrance." My head was

starting to throb from the smell. The sooner I got out in the fresh air, the better. "Ishtar, I am going for a walk before breakfast. Come with me."

"Of course, Sister," she said in a voice that was so meek it didn't even sound like her own.

As we left my chamber with her following behind me, I took a deep breath and tried to push away my lingering resentment. She was in enough pain without me making it worse.

"Please don't act like a servant," I said. "Come walk beside me. We can't talk when you walk behind me like that."

She came to walk with me without comment and we made our way through the Palace. I nodded to women I recognised and said good morning to the few I had actually met. Every day I noticed faces I hadn't seen before. I hadn't heard of any new Ornaments arriving — and surely Tiye would have said something if that had happened as we would no longer need to pretend I still cleaned her bathing chamber — so presumably these were simply other residents I hadn't yet met. There were so many of us here, after all. It shouldn't be surprising I still saw women who were new to me.

We emerged outside and my eyes burned from the brightness after the dimness of the hallways. The sky was a deep azure blue without a single cloud to mar its expanse. I hadn't yet seen a cloudy day, let alone a rainy one. The air was already warm, hinting at the heat to come.

"Did you know every day is like this?" I asked Ishtar. "Hot and clear."

"Wait until the rainy season. You'll forgot the hot, clear days then."

"That's just it. There is no rainy season. The Great River

floods once a year and when the waters go back down, the farmers plant their crops in the silt it leaves behind."

"But where does the water come from if it doesn't rain? If the river floods, it must receive rain somewhere."

"I don't know," I admitted. "I never thought to ask."

We walked in silence for a while. I hoped Ishtar might try to make conversation, but she said nothing. I searched for something else we could talk about.

"It is very beautiful here," I said. "Not just these gardens. The wild areas we passed through as we sailed were beautiful too."

"I suppose. It is nothing like Babylon, though."

"I try not to compare them. I will probably never see Babylon again, so there is no point in thinking such things."

"I'm sorry," she said.

"Ishtar, please stop apologising."

"I'm—" She swallowed down the rest.

"We need to find a way to make this situation work," I said. "For better or worse, we are both here now and I should think each of us is grateful to have a sister with us."

"I am grateful I am not here alone."

Her voice trembled and I was surprised at the irritation that rose within me. Ishtar had never been uncertain about anything and this new version of her irked me. I wanted my confident sister back. The one who didn't cry and apologise all the time. The one who smiled and sparkled and had never been uncertain of herself in her whole life. Patience, I told myself. She has had a terrible time these past few months and whatever happened with Pharaoh has broken her. It is hardly any wonder she is not as you remember.

"There is a man over there," Ishtar said suddenly.

I looked in the direction she nodded and could just make

out a figure hidden in the shadows of a stand of dom palm trees. I tucked my arm through Ishtar's and tried to look unconcerned. If we were holding onto each other, surely neither of us could be dragged away.

"Keep walking," I said. "And don't look at him. The path turns just past him and we will be back in a more open area after that. He must be a guard, or maybe a servant."

My heart pounded as we drew nearer to the man. What if he was hiding because he wasn't supposed to be here? Should we turn back? But the spot ahead of us where the dom palm trees and the shrubs gave way to flower gardens and open swathes of grass was no more than thirty paces and the nearest such place behind us was twice that distance.

I inhaled deeply and tried to steady myself. Ten more paces and we would be past him, then another twenty paces to safety. My heart pounded so hard Ishtar must surely be able to hear it.

As we drew closer to the man, he spoke.

"Lady Kassaya."

I was so surprised to hear my name that I stopped walking and peered into the shadows, trying to see who it was.

"Sutem?" I asked.

"Khaemmalu," he said. "Come closer. I don't want to risk anyone seeing us together. Stand in front of the dom palm and pretend you are resting while you chat with your sister."

"How did you know she is my sister?" I asked as I tugged Ishtar's arm to move her to the spot he indicated.

"Kassaya," she hissed at me. "It isn't safe."

"It is all right," I said. "He is one of the guards. Do as he says."

I hadn't seen Khaemmalu since the night I arrived. Did he

remember how it sounded like I was flirting with him? Against my will, my cheeks heated at the memory. Marduk!

Khaemmalu waited until Ishtar and I were positioned as he wanted before he spoke again, although he didn't answer my question.

"Your maid," he said. "Ettu."

"You have news of her?" Forgetting his instructions, I turned to him.

"Face away," he said quickly. "You have merely stopped to rest. Pretend you are admiring the flowers over there."

Obediently, I pointed towards some flowers and commented loudly to Ishtar on how pretty they were. She nodded vigorously in agreement. Still clutching her arm, I could feel how she trembled.

"Ettu left the Palace grounds last night," Khaemmalu said.

"I wouldn't know anything about that." I turned towards Ishtar as I spoke, trying to appear as if I was talking to her.

"Oh, I'm sure you do," he said. "I'd be interested to know how she did it. I saw her walk out right under the noses of the guards. They didn't stop her."

"I suppose the guards must have been bribed then."

"No, I don't believe they were. I spoke to them afterwards. Asked if anyone had left and they swore they had seen nobody since the start of their shift other than a messenger."

"If they were bribed, they would hardly admit it."

"I'm pretty good at knowing when someone lies to me," Khaemmalu said. "And the guards weren't lying. You, on the other hand…"

"If you are so sure my maid left the grounds, what have you done about it? Have you reported her?"

"Not yet. I'd like to know the reason for her departure

before I decide whether to report her. And how she walked out so brazenly."

I debated what to do. He already knew I was lying. Could I convince him not to report her?

"Do you know where she is?" I asked. "She didn't come back."

"I haven't seen her since she left. I thought she might be running away."

I took a deep breath and decided to trust him. Not with the whole truth, but a part of it.

"She was delivering a message for me," I admitted. "One I couldn't risk the Palace scribe deciding not to forward."

"And did you expect her to have returned by now?"

"I did. I am very worried she hasn't."

"Who was she to deliver this message to?"

I tried to think of a reply that wouldn't give him too much information.

"You can trust me, Lady Kassaya," he added when I hesitated. "I can help you."

"Or you can report me." I nudged Ishtar and gestured again to some flowers, trying to maintain our facade in case anyone was watching.

"Which I have not done," Khaemmalu said.

"Why? What benefit is it to you to know such a thing and not report it?"

Did he mean to have something to blackmail me with? That was the only reason I could think of.

"You haven't been here long and I'm sure there is much you have yet to learn about the Palace," he said, "but surely you have discovered there are alliances to be made? Who you ally yourself with can determine your fate here."

"You make it sound very dramatic," I said. "The alliances these women have are hardly a matter of life and death."

"They may well be," he said. "Someday."

"That all sounds very mysterious, but it doesn't help my maid. If there is something you can do for her, tell me plainly."

"I would, if you would tell me plainly where she went."

When I didn't reply, he continued.

"I took Sutem's shift so I could be here today to watch for her return," he said. "I work nights. So that means I was on duty last night and I'm here all day today and then my usual shift tonight. Do you think I would do such a thing if I didn't think it was important?"

"All that because you saw Ettu leave?"

"You have been here long enough to understand the significance. Nobody who resides in the Palace leaves — ever — without Pharaoh's express permission. Like your sister there. She went out a few nights ago at his request. But unlike your maid, the guards were advised in advance of her departure and, also unlike your maid, she returned."

Was he staring at Ishtar? Captivated by her beauty? Mindful we were supposed to be admiring the flowers, I didn't let myself turn to see, but I could feel his curiosity about her.

"Ishtar, this is Khaemmalu," I said, pointing towards another flower bed as if I was commenting on them. "As you've probably figured by now, he's a night duty guard."

Ishtar nodded, but said nothing.

"Ishtar," he said, perhaps committing her name to memory. "Well? How did Ettu just walk out?"

"I can't tell you." There was no point pretending I didn't know what he was talking about. "It is better if you don't know the details anyway."

"So where is she? I assume if she hasn't returned, there's a possibility she is in trouble."

"A strong possibility, unfortunately." I kept my gaze on the flowers we were supposed to be admiring.

"I can search for her after I finish work, but that won't be until dawn tomorrow."

"You can't possibly go looking for her after you've worked three shifts in a row."

Besides, if Ettu hadn't returned by then, something was seriously wrong. For now, I could cling to the hope she had merely been delayed and couldn't get past the guards before the potion wore off. Ahmose could go out tonight and check the place where Ettu was supposed to wait if she couldn't get back inside. I didn't know what we would do if she wasn't there. I couldn't let myself think about the possibility that she, like Nebtu, might have disappeared without a trace.

"Who else will go search for her?" Khaemmalu asked. "Oh, you think another of your servants can walk right out past the guards."

I shifted my gaze to a different flowering bush, thankful he couldn't see my face which undoubtedly revealed my guilt.

"We will search for her ourselves," I said.

"Do you, like your servants, have the ability to walk past the guards undetected?"

"Don't be ridiculous." I pointed towards the flower bush and nudged Ishtar, as if commenting on it to her. She nodded, but didn't even pretend to reply.

"I know what I saw. If the guards weren't bribed, then some kind of magic was used against them."

"Magic," I scoffed and hoped it sounded more genuine to his ear than mine. "Do you really believe such a thing?"

"I know what I saw," he repeated. "And I can think of only two possibilities."

A low whistle sounded, barely audible.

"Go," Khaemmalu said. "Someone is coming. If you don't find Ettu tonight, send one of your servants to find me before dawn and I will look for her."

By the time I turned towards him, he had already disappeared further into the shadows. Even though I knew he was still there, I couldn't see him.

"Come, Ishtar," I said loudly, for the benefit anyone who might be within hearing distance. "We have dallied too long, regardless of the beauty of the flowers here."

We walked on, trying to maintain the appearance of a casual stroll.

CHAPTER 19

I knew we didn't need to be afraid of whoever was approaching with Khaemmalu watching from the shadows. Even if I couldn't see him anymore, I could still feel his eyes on us.

"I didn't understand half of what he said," Ishtar said.

"Shh," I whispered. "Not now."

Footsteps on the path behind us. The whisper of sandals against mud bricks. A female voice called a cheery good morning. It was Gilukhipa, trailed this time by two maids.

"Gilukhipa," I said with a nod. "Good morning."

"Will we see you at Ineni's gathering tonight?" she asked as she drew alongside me. "I asked you last time, but it was only after we parted that I realised you never answered."

We set off down the path together. Ishtar dropped back to walk behind us, although when I glanced at her, she walked alone, ahead of Gilukhipa's maids. If Ettu or Merytre were with me, they would walk with the maids and take the opportunity to get any news from them.

"Yes, of course," I said. "Do you know who else will be there?"

"Ineni, obviously." Gilukhipa counted off the names on her fingers. "Henutmire. Neferu. I don't know whether you have met her yet? She eats in a different dining chamber, so you wouldn't have encountered her at breakfast."

"No, I haven't."

"You, me, Tiye. That is everyone."

"Tiye is going?"

I wouldn't have expected her to deign to attend such a small and private gathering.

"That surprises you?" Gilukhipa asked, giving me a sideways glance. "It was Tiye who told Ineni to invite you. We five are a small and quite… intimate group. A newcomer would have to prove herself before we trusted her. But Tiye's good opinion at least gets you in the door."

"How would I go about proving myself?"

"Oh, there is no need to worry about such things right now. Just come to Ineni's tonight and let us get to know you."

So tonight was to be a test of sorts. Tiye might have decided to trust me, but the others hadn't yet. I hoped she had told all of them I didn't steal her jewels. Should I say something about it to Gilukhipa? But I sensed no hesitation from her, so if folk were still calling me a thief, it seemed she didn't believe it. Better not to remind her of something she might have already forgotten.

"I will see you then," Gilukhipa said. "Farewell for now."

She hurried away down the path and her maids followed. Ishtar came to walk beside me again.

"That sounded very mysterious," she said.

As I started to respond, I suddenly realised it mightn't be prudent to share too much with her. She already knew things she might reveal to Pharaoh, either inadvertently or to gain favour with him. Maybe to stop him from hurting her anymore. Now she had his ear, we should be cautious about how much she knew. I didn't like to think such things about Ishtar, but I wasn't sure I could afford not to. She already knew we were sneaking out of the grounds.

"It was hardly mysterious," I said. "Just a small gathering of Ornaments tonight. I don't know any of them well and it will be good to have the chance to get to know them better."

"You must be looking forward to it."

Her voice was envious and I tried to squash the resentment that rose within me.

"It will be a pleasant diversion," I said.

Even if she asked outright, I wouldn't take her with me. But that wasn't Ishtar's way. She would hint at it, if indeed that was what she wanted, but she would never ask directly.

Sweat trickled down the back of my neck and I noticed how much hotter it was than when we first came out. We must have been talking to Khaemmalu for longer than I realised.

"Let's go back," I said. "Merytre and Ahmose will be worried by now."

"I can't imagine there is a safer place in all of Egypt. As you've already seen, there are guards hiding in the bushes, and look at that great wall all around us."

"Have you not heard about Nebtu's disappearance?"

My voice was sharp, but Ishtar's naivety surprised me. Had she listened to nothing of what we discussed in my chambers?

"That was one woman," Ishtar said. "And we know she returned to her father's home."

I only shook my head. Did she really not understand the administrators were lying, or did she just not *want* to believe?

Perhaps I didn't need to worry about her telling Pharaoh the things she knew after all.

"Did you say anything to Pharaoh about Nebtu?" I asked.

Please Marduk, let Ishtar have had the sense to tell him a woman was missing, even if she relayed the tale about her returning home.

"Of course not. I'm hardly going to…" Her voice trailed away as if she had suddenly realised that whatever she had meant to say, was probably best not said to me.

"Go on."

"I'm not going to remind him about other women. Not while I'm alone with him."

"Does he even remember you aren't an Ornament?"

I kept my gaze on the path ahead of us. Mud bricks, smoothed by countless feet. How many women had wandered this path? How many alliances had been made on it? Confidences shared? Secrets revealed?

"I have said nothing about it," she admitted. "Only…"

"Just say it, Ishtar."

It could hardly be any worse than what she had already done.

"I only told him I don't have my own chambers."

"And I suppose he said he would see to that?"

"He didn't say. But he asked how many lady's maids I had."

"And you told him you had none because you weren't an Ornament." My voice was heavy with sarcasm.

"No." Her words were little more than a whisper and I had to strain to hear them. "I said I had no maids."

"Of course you did." Was that before or after he hurt her?

"I'm sorry to have displeased you, Sister."

"Don't. We both know you would never be satisfied with being a maid. I can't believe Father thought you would."

"He didn't care whether I wanted this." Her voice was tearful. "He didn't care whether I would be happy. The only thing he cared about was the alliance."

"You think I don't know that?" I snapped. "Remember who got sent here when you got yourself with child? Father didn't care whether I would be happy and neither did you."

"Sister," she whispered.

"Don't," I said again. "I can't even bear to talk to you right now."

I walked faster, striding ahead of her. She didn't try to catch up with me and we returned to the Palace like that, with me walking ahead of my sister.

CHAPTER 20

Back in my chambers, I told Merytre and Ahmose what Khaemmalu said. I glanced at Ishtar from time to time, wondering whether she might add something — a comment I had forgotten to relay? something I misremembered? — but she said nothing, only stared at her hands in her lap and didn't even seem to be listening.

When the time came to prepare me for Ineni's gathering, I managed to convince Merytre not to send for the rest of my maids.

"It is only six women," I said. "Hardly worth drawing them all away from their sewing and weaving to attend to me."

Merytre frowned, but eventually agreed that for a gathering of six, she could manage my appearance, even without Ettu. But before she could start dressing me, Panouk arrived at the door, bursting with obsequiousness and self-importance, to usher Ishtar to her own chambers. She told him to send for Belet-ili to be her lady's maid and I was immediately sorry I never got around to asking for her to be assigned to cleaning or cooking when I didn't need her, as I had planned.

Ishtar said nothing to any of us as she left, not even a farewell to me, or a thank you for giving her a bedchamber.

"An interesting development," Ahmose said after Ishtar and Panouk were gone. I could feel her studying me while she decided what else to say. "How do you feel about Ishtar being given her own chambers?"

I tried to look unconcerned.

"The only thing that surprises me is that she didn't manage to do it sooner," I said.

How would Ettu feel when she returned and learned Ishtar took Belet-ili and not her? And why didn't Ishtar ask for her as well? Maybe Ettu had told her about the agreement we made.

"I suppose that means she is an Ornament now," Merytre said. "We will have to call her Lady Ishtar."

"Have you ever heard of such a thing before?" I asked. "A servant being elevated to Ornament?"

"Oh, yes. She is not the first. I have never known it to happen so quickly, though. Normally a woman would have to work much harder to get herself into the position of Ornament."

I made a non-committal noise and hoped she would take it for agreement.

"I am sure Belet-ili will be pleased to be serving her again," Merytre said. "I wonder if she will ask for Nammu as well?"

"Would Nammu even go to her if she asks? Right now she serves Pharaoh's Favourite. Ishtar is no more than the newest Ornament. Wouldn't Nammu lose status if she were to transfer to Ishtar?"

"As Belet-ili surely does," Merytre said. "After all, as the newest Ornament, Lady Ishtar is of lower status than you."

I hadn't thought of it like that. Was there any possibility

Belet-ili would refuse to serve Ishtar? Was she even permitted to refuse? And would anyone ask my permission for her to be reassigned?

"If Belet-ili won't go willingly, I will send her myself," I said.

Merytre dressed me in a gown made of the palest blue linen. She paired it with a wig of many dozens of tiny braids, threaded with silver and blue baubles. A long length of blue beads was wound several times around my neck and my wrists were heavy with golden bangles. At least I was able to convince her I didn't need the scented oils to be reapplied, or any perfume. This morning's applications had only just faded enough for my nose to stop running.

Merytre made up my face with heavy lines of kohl around my eyes and a red paste on my lips and cheeks. When she passed me the hand mirror to inspect her work, I hardly recognised myself.

"That is much more makeup than I usually wear," I said, somewhat doubtfully. "I fear I am overdressed for such a small gathering."

"Quite the contrary, my lady," she said. "They will all be wearing their best. It might be a small group, and maybe they view themselves more as friends than competitors, but it is still a chance to dress up and show off a new gown or wig."

Merytre and Ahmose walked me to Ineni's chambers. They waited while I knocked on the door and when Ineni opened it, they slipped away.

"Kassaya, welcome," Ineni said. "Come in."

"Thank you," I said. "You look very beautiful."

One glance at Ineni told me Merytre was correct in thinking the women would wear their finest. Her gown was a shimmery white and trailed behind her as she walked. A silver chain emphasised her slim waist, its links a match for the more delicate chains around her wrists.

Ineni's couches had been pushed back against the walls to make room for an assortment of low tables and cushions, which looked much like those from the dining chamber. A long bench along one wall bore trays of food and bottles of wine. The lamps were turned down low, creating a more intimate atmosphere.

"Am I the first to arrive?" I asked. "Am I too early?"

"No, no, you are just in time," Ineni said. "Everyone else will be along soon enough. In the meantime, pour yourself some wine. I borrowed the furniture from the dining chamber, as you might guess. Panouk hates it when I do that, but he can hardly come and take it back while we are using it."

She picked up a mug from one of the tables and took a quick sip. Someone knocked at the door and she set the mug down again.

"Oh, here we go," she said.

I poured some wine while she let in a woman whose face was vaguely familiar. I guessed I must have passed her in the hallways. As Ineni introduced us, my gaze was drawn to the strange pendant Neferu wore on a chain around her neck. A stylised eye, which seemed to stare right at me. It sent a shiver through me and I focussed my gaze on Neferu's face, trying not to look at the pendant. Neferu gave me an appraising look up and down.

"So, you are Ishtar's sister," she said. "If she is half as beautiful as you, I can see why she has entranced Pharaoh so. He has always had a weakness for exotic beauties."

I sipped my wine while I tried to find a reply that would be more polite than a scoff. Neferu obviously hadn't seen Ishtar herself or she wouldn't compare us like that.

"Ishtar is indeed a rare beauty," Ineni said. "I saw her walking in the gardens with Kassaya. There can be no doubt they are sisters."

"She is beautiful," I said, unable to come up with anything else. I had grown up hearing comments about Ishtar's appearance, so this was no more than I was used to. "Neferu, your necklace is…"

My voice trailed away as I tried to find a way to describe the pendant without revealing the dread it filled me with.

"An Eye of Horus," Neferu said, without waiting for me to finish.

"It feels like it is staring at me."

"It is for protection. Imbued with spells to deter evil."

"That sounds very serious." And sinister.

"We have all been wearing protective amulets since Nebtu disappeared." Ineni held out her hand to show me the finger ring she wore. It too bore the strange eye which seemed to stare right at me. "You don't have one?"

"No, I have never seen anything like it before," I said.

"I have a spare amulet," Neferu said. "I will send it to your chambers tomorrow."

"You are too kind." I didn't want to offend her, but I didn't think I could bear to wear anything with that ghastly eye on it.

Someone knocked and Ineni went to open the door again.

"Where are Ineni's maids?" I asked. "Are they not here to answer the door for her?"

"She sent them away for the evening," Neferu said. "We always send the maids away. One cannot speak of private things with servants listening in the background."

Henutmire and Gilukhipa arrived and greeted me cheerfully. If anyone still believed I had stolen Tiye's jewels, they were pretending it didn't bother them, for tonight at least. Tiye was the last to arrive, sweeping in without even bothering to knock.

"Fashionably late, as always," Ineni said cheerfully, seemingly unbothered she had let herself in.

"Of course," Tiye replied. "Would you expect me to be early?"

"Kassaya was," Ineni said. "She was the first to arrive."

My cheeks heated and I hoped the lamplight was low enough to conceal them.

"I didn't know when to come," I muttered.

The women chattered as they poured themselves wine and piled plates with food. I hung back, suddenly feeling shy and awkward. From the joking insults and the laughter at half-said comments, it was clear they knew each other intimately. Although I followed most of what they said well enough, I didn't understand all the jokes. Maybe the humour was lost by the time I figured out what had been said, even though my grasp of their language improved every day, or maybe they were only funny if one knew the stories behind them.

I found myself envying their intimacy. I had never had women friends like this. Had never been part of a group with shared jokes and a common history. Maybe the next time I attended such a gathering, I would be one of the insiders. Maybe eventually there would be another new woman, lingering in the corner and wondering whether she would ever be accepted.

"Kassaya, hurry up and get some food before these beasts eat it all." Ineni tugged my arm, pulling me from my thoughts. "Go on, get yourself a plate. As you might have noticed, there are no servants tonight. If you want to eat, you will have to serve yourself."

Ineni had arranged a marvellous variety of food. There was roasted hens, whole baked fish, a root vegetable I didn't recognise, and a large dish of the crunchy sweet onions the Egyptians seemed to favour. Several types of bread, cheese — both soft and hard — lentils, and an assortment of fruits. I took a modest serving, although my stomach grumbled fiercely. I didn't want to look greedy, but when I glanced around as I settled myself on a cushion, I realised the other women had no such compunctions. Their plates were piled high and some even had a second plate of food already waiting on their table.

"Wine?" Ineni topped up my mug without waiting for a reply, then bustled off to check everyone else's drinks.

I gnawed the meat from a hen's leg as I listened to the conversation. It seemed to be mostly gossip from around the Palace and each of the women had some contribution to make. Neferu relayed a story about a kitchen maid who was caught stealing bread and Tiye knew of two Ornaments who were newly engaged in an affair. She named them both, but I knew neither. The other women laughed and nobody seemed particularly shocked.

I supposed such affairs must happen regularly since we had no contact with the outside world. If a woman was lonely, there were only the other residents to spend time with. I didn't let myself think about the guards, knowing my cheeks would go bright red at the memory of Khaemmalu thinking I was flirting.

Gilukhipa told us about finding a cat that had somehow made its way into the Palace and the antics that ensued when she tried to catch it.

"If you wanted a cat, it would have been easier to tell Panouk to fetch you one," Ineni said.

"I know," Gilukhipa said. "But I wanted *that* cat. It had the sweetest face."

The cat, it seemed, didn't want her and was determined not to be caught. The story ended with Gilukhipa empty-handed and the cat going on its way.

"What about you, Kassaya?" Henutmire asked when they had each relayed their gossip. "What news do you have?"

Caught licking the last of the grease off my fingers, I tried to pretend I wasn't blushing as they all turned their attention to me. For a moment I wondered whether I should tell them Ettu was missing. Maybe one of them would know something useful. But I wasn't yet sure who I could trust other than maybe Henutmire.

"I don't have anything to share," I said. "I'm afraid I haven't met enough people here to know any gossip yet."

"Tell them about what happened when you stole my jewels." Tiye's voice was light and she gave me a grin that seemed unusually open for her.

"Oh, go on," Ineni said. "I have heard whispers about it, but not the whole story."

Hesitantly, I told them about Nammu stealing Tiye's finger ring and planting it in my clothing chest. Her disappointment when she went to retrieve it in front of the other maids, only to find it gone. Then how she gave Panouk another jewel she had stolen and claimed to have found it in one of my chests. How Panouk searched my chambers, locked me up, and eventually found the finger ring in Ettu's pouch.

The women reacted with gasps and I caught more than one mutter about what they would have done to Nammu if she was their maid.

"Is it true you took her on as your own maid after that?" Henutmire asked Tiye.

"I did," Tiye said. "And she still thinks I believe Kassaya stole the jewels and forced her maid to conceal it and suffer the consequences."

"She can't know Kassaya all that well then," Henutmire said. "I myself have only spoken to her a few times, but already I could tell you she is not the type who would make a maid bear the punishment for something she had done herself."

"I knew there was more to the tale as soon as I heard about it," Gilukhipa declared. "It all sounded like nonsense to me."

Ineni said nothing and I remembered the way she had turned her back to me. She, at least, had thought I was guilty and I hadn't been surprised. I hadn't thought anyone would take my side even before they heard what had really happened. She must have changed her mind now, though, or surely she wouldn't have invited me tonight, even with Tiye's urging. She wouldn't want a thief in her chambers.

"Are we going to talk business?" Henutmire asked, her voice more serious now.

"Not tonight," Tiye said, shooting a look in my direction.

"I thought we decided to trust her?" Henutmire asked and was quickly shushed by one of the others.

I took a long drink of my wine and pretended I hadn't heard. What "business" was it they wanted to talk about that they didn't trust me to hear? Ineni got up to offer around more wine and the conversation turned back to lighter matters.

CHAPTER 21

Ineni's gathering lasted until late into the night. My eyes drooped and I was trying not to yawn long before anyone suggested it might be time to leave. I didn't want to be the first to depart, but the later we talked, the more I fretted over whether Ahmose was waiting for me to return before she went looking for Ettu. As we finally left, Ineni surprised me with a kiss on the cheek.

"Thank you for coming," she said. "I hope you weren't too bored. We must have spent a lot of time talking about people you don't know."

I emerged into the hallway to find a line of maids waiting to escort their mistress to her chambers. So I wasn't the only one taking measures to ensure I didn't walk the hallways alone. Ahmose and Merytre were there, leaning against the wall and looking more awake than I felt. We didn't speak until we were well away from anyone else.

"Is there any news?" I asked, rubbing my eyes and trying to look alert. "Ahmose, I thought you would have gone by now."

"I was waiting until we collected you before I left," Ahmose said. "So Merytre wouldn't have to come on her own."

"I'm sorry I was so long," I said. "I should have made an excuse to leave earlier."

"Did you learn anything useful?" Merytre asked.

We reached my chambers and I tried to pretend to myself I wasn't hoping Ettu would be there when we opened the door. She wasn't, of course. I waited until the door closed behind us before I answered Merytre.

"It was mostly Palace gossip, but there is some kind of alliance between the women who were there," I said. "Henut-mire asked whether they were going to talk business, and then something about how she thought they had decided to trust me. I don't know what it was all about."

"Interesting," Merytre said.

Ahmose disappeared into her bedchamber to prepare to leave. I sank down onto a couch, lightheaded as fatigue and too much wine both caught up with me.

"Do you think she is all right?" The words slipped out before I realised what I was going to say.

Merytre sighed. "I don't know and that's the truth. I pray to Horus she is well."

"Funny you should mention Horus," I said and told her about the protective amulets the women were wearing.

"I have one myself, although I don't wear it on a chain." Merytre fumbled in her pouch and withdrew a small item. She set it on her palm and held out her hand to show me. Like the ones I had seen earlier, the eye seemed to stare at me balefully.

"You don't find it... disturbing?" I resisted the urge to edge away from it.

"Of course not." Merytre tucked it back in her pouch. "It

protects me from evil. That's why I'm not afraid to walk the hallways alone. I did tell Ahmose she didn't need to wait tonight because Horus would protect me, but she insisted."

"I'm surprised everyone wasn't already wearing such amulets. Didn't you say Nebtu isn't the first Ornament to have disappeared?"

"No, not the first. I suppose she might be the first these particular women knew personally, though. That must make them more discomfited than previously. As for me, I have had this for years. We should get one for Ettu, and Ahmose too if she doesn't have one."

Ahmose returned before I could reply.

"I will try to be back before the guards change at dawn," she said. "But don't worry if I am not. If I am delayed, it most likely means I have found some sign of Ettu. If there is nothing, I will come straight back."

"Please be careful," I said. "I really don't like you going out alone like this."

"Oh, I am safe enough," she said. "Nobody would bother stealing an old woman. They don't even see me most of the time."

Merytre restrained a yawn as she offered to walk Ahmose to the gates, but the woman waved her away and slipped out the door.

"Go to bed," I said to Merytre, sinking back into the couch and trying to look more alert than I felt. "I'll wait for her."

"You can't sit up every night," she protested, settling herself in a chair and looking like she was not inclined to get up again. "Let me take a turn. I swear I won't leave this chamber until they are back and I'll wake you the moment they are here."

A great yawn washed over me and suddenly I could hardly keep my eyes open.

"Maybe just for an hour or two," I said.

I stumbled off to my bedchamber. It seemed like far too much effort to undress, so I climbed into bed as I was and fell asleep almost before I lay down. After what felt like mere minutes, I swam up from a deep sleep and dozed on and off for a while before I managed to peel open my eyes. The chamber was bathed with light and the bird that usually sang its dawn song outside my window was silent. It must be long after sunrise. Why didn't Merytre wake me?

I rose and almost fell back into my bed when the chamber seemed to spin around me. I clutched the bed frame while I waited for the spinning to stop. My head pounded and I wanted nothing more than to crawl back into bed and stay there for another few hours. I shouldn't have let Ineni fill my mug so many times.

I tried to straighten my gown, but there was no way to make it look like I hadn't slept in it. When I entered the sitting chamber, Merytre was fast asleep on the couch.

"Merytre?"

She sat up quickly.

"Oh, my lady," she said. "I must have just dozed off. I sat up all night and the last thing I remember was the sun starting to rise."

"Are they not back yet?"

"Not unless they slipped in after I fell asleep. Wait here and I will check their bedchambers."

She was gone for only a few moments and returned shaking her head. My heart sank. Had Ahmose been caught? No, she said if she was delayed it would be because she had found some sign of Ettu. I had to trust that was true.

"I need to go out to the gardens," I said.

Khaemmalu had said to send a message to him before dawn. Was there any chance he was still there?

"Now?" Merytre eyed my gown. "You need to change first, and your kohl is smudged all over your face. You can't go wandering outside like that."

"There is no time. I have to find Khaemmalu."

"I can go for you," she said. "You will draw too much attention if you go out like that."

I told her where Khaemmalu had said he would wait.

"Please be careful," I said as she left. All I could do now was pray to Marduk that Khaemmalu was still there.

While I waited for Merytre, I found a jug of washing water which was still half full and tried to clean the makeup from my face. I set my wig on its shelf and changed into a nightgown. At least when my maids came to dress me, it wouldn't look like I had gone to bed fully clothed. They arrived soon after and it was almost a relief to be surrounded by their bustle and chatter. At least it distracted me from my worries.

"My lady, where are Ettu and Merytre?" one asked as they sat me on the stool in the bathing chamber and poured warm water over me.

"They have gone for a walk."

It was the first thing that popped into my head. Why didn't I think to prepare an explanation? Of course their absence would be noticed. If anyone doubted two of my maids would be out walking so early and before I was dressed, none of them said it. As they bathed me, I busied myself with worrying about Ettu and Ahmose. When I next tuned into their chatter, I realised I should have been paying more attention.

"Did you hear Lady Tiye has summoned her?" one of the women asked.

Others laughed or murmured agreement.

"You know what that means," someone else said.

"What does it mean?" I asked as I tried to figure out which one had said it.

"You know," one of the women said. "Lady Tiye does this with every new Ornament. But of course, you are the only one who has ever refused."

"It will be interesting to see if Lady Ishtar does," someone said.

"Oh, no, she won't. She's not the type."

"Hush. You forget Lady Ishtar is my lady's sister."

"Oh, of course."

"My lady, forgive us."

I closed my eyes and pretended I wasn't listening anymore. So Tiye had called for Ishtar. That could only mean one thing. She was back to her old trick of demanding the new Ornament clean her bathing chamber.

CHAPTER 22

By the time the women finished dressing me, Merytre had returned alone. I waited for someone to ask why Ettu wasn't with her, since they had supposedly gone walking together, but nobody did. Perhaps they thought better of it since the situation was so odd.

"Well?" I asked as the door finally closed behind my departing maids.

"I found him," she said. "He made a point of telling me he said he would only wait until dawn."

"It was good of him to wait, but will he look for them?"

"I told him where Ettu was supposed to go if she couldn't get back in. Of course, he asked how she got out in the first place. I pretended I knew nothing more than that she hadn't returned. I told him Ahmose had gone to find her and hadn't come back either."

"How will he let us know if he has any news?" I sat on a couch, careless about whether my skirt would crease. How could I be concerned about such a thing at a time like this?

"I am to meet him in the same place at noon."

"I suppose all we can do now is wait," I said.

"What if he does find them? He can hardly bring them back into the grounds without the guards knowing."

"We will figure something out." I hadn't thought that far ahead. My only concern had been finding Ettu.

"We might need some help," Merytre said.

"Are you suggesting we tell Khaemmalu how they got out?" I leaned back against the couch and eyed her.

"No," she said. "Yes. I don't know."

"Ahmose will have extra potion ingredients with her. She anticipated she might be delayed, and she will have enough to get them both back in."

Merytre only frowned, seemingly not convinced that would be sufficient.

"I don't know Khaemmalu well enough to know whether we can trust him," I said.

"What about the women you dined with last night? Is there one of them you can trust?"

Henutmire, maybe. Perhaps even Tiye.

"I don't know," I said. "I don't think we should risk it. Let's wait and see what news Khaemmalu has. We can decide then."

The rest of the morning passed slowly with our only distraction being the arrival of two of Neferu's maids. They handed Merytre a small item wrapped in linen, saying it was with their lady's compliments, and hurried off.

"I suppose this is for you." Merytre offered me the package.

"Neferu said she would send me an Eye of Horus."

I opened the wrappings and stared down at the Eye nestled within them. It was a fine piece, made of lapis lazuli, its pupil a deep red gem. Just like the others I had seen, it sent a shiver through me.

"I am not sure I can bear to wear it," I said.

I plucked the Eye out of its wrappings and held it up to show Merytre. I had expected it to be cool, but it was warm and I would have sworn it vibrated as I touched it. I quickly dropped it back onto the linen.

"You can carry it in your pouch," Merytre said. "But folk say the amulet is most effective if you wear it against your skin."

"Then why don't you wear yours?"

"I used to, but the cord kept breaking. I tried wearing it around my neck and also around my wrist. After I lost it twice, I gave up and have kept it in my pouch ever since."

"I shall do the same. I really don't think I can wear it."

I tucked it away in the little pouch I wore around my waist, like the Egyptian women did. It was a handy thing. A place to store small items I needed to carry, or something I had found. I wasn't sure I believed the amulet had any mystical power to protect me, but it couldn't hurt to carry it so long as I didn't have to see it.

As the sun reached its peak, Merytre and I went to meet Khaemmalu. We walked slowly, trying to give the appearance we were simply out for a midday stroll. I made a show of pointing out various flowers and Merytre did a much better job than Ishtar of pretending to admire them. I tried not to let myself worry about what he had learned.

A bush rustled as we approached the spot where Khaemmalu was to wait and I figured that was his way of letting us know he was there. It made me wonder how often I passed a hidden guard who held still and gave away no sign of his presence. Merytre and I leaned against a couple of dom palms and pretended we were resting.

"I found them," Khaemmalu said before I could ask. "There

was trouble, but they are well enough. It would seem they don't have a way of getting back inside, though. Ahmose said you would know what that meant."

"Tell me what happened," I said, resisting the urge to turn around. He would have come out from behind the bushes if he wanted to be seen. It was better if nobody suspected I was talking to anyone other than Merytre beside me.

"Ettu is fine. She was simply delayed returning — something about having to take a different route and losing her way in the dark — so she went to the place she was supposed to wait if there was a problem. Ahmose, however, was accosted on her way there. She has a broken wrist and her sack was stolen. She said you should gather everything you can find and put it in another sack. I assume you understand whatever that means. I will take it to her and apparently this will somehow allow them to get back in tonight."

"So they are both safe." The relief that surged through me was immense. I hadn't realised until this moment just how afraid I had been for Ettu.

Merytre clutched my arm and I wondered whether it was because she suddenly found herself unsteady on her feet, or if she realised I had. I shook my head to clear my thoughts.

"Thank you," I said to Khaemmalu. "You have done me a great service today."

"It would seem my service is not yet complete." His voice was wry and I wished I could see what expression his face held.

"I'm sorry to ask you for more, but there is nobody else I can trust with this." I nudged Merytre and smiled, trying to pretend we shared a joke.

"But you don't trust me enough to tell me what was in

Ahmose's sack which allows them to walk right past the guards at the gates."

"It's… complicated," I said.

"Sounds like magic to me."

"Do you intend to turn me in?" I held my breath as I waited for his reply.

"To Amankhau?" I heard him spit at the ground, surprising me with his vehemence. "That snake. No, I'll gladly help your women get back inside if only to spite Amankhau."

"Thank you. Can you give me an hour to find what Ahmose needs? I will come right back."

"I will be waiting," he said. A dry leaf crunched underfoot as he slipped away.

Merytre and I walked briskly back to the Palace.

"I think you can trust him," she said.

"Me too. I hope I am not wrong."

I once thought I could trust Ishtar, but had since discovered I wasn't a very good judge of character. I could only pray to Marduk that Khaemmalu didn't betray me. It wasn't just me who would be endangered if he did, but all those who shared my chambers. But I couldn't think of any other way we might get Ahmose's ingredients to her since nobody else knew how to make her potion. Without our own dose, neither Merytre nor I could get out to her. Once Ahmose was safely back inside, I would insist she show me how to make it myself.

Back in my suite, Merytre found a sack while I searched Ahmose's bedchamber. She had few personal belongings and it took me only moments to find a small chest which contained dozens of little linen packages arranged in tidy rows.

"I suppose what she needs is in here," I said as Merytre came in with the sack.

She peered over my shoulder.

"There are an awful lot of packets in there." Her voice was doubtful. "How will we know which ones she needs?"

"Has she ever told you what is in her potion?"

"No, but I never asked either."

"I did, and she wouldn't say. I wouldn't know what any of these are anyway, so I suppose we just send it all. She will have to figure out which ones she needs."

We studied the packets.

"Nothing is labelled," Merytre said. "What if they are in some sort of order that tells her what they are? Maybe she won't know which is which if they get mixed up."

I picked up a packet and peeked inside. It contained little round seeds, light brown in colour. Another packet held dried pieces of something that looked like grass. A third had more little round seeds which were no more than a shade or two darker than the others. Surely they were similar enough to be easily confused with the first packet.

"What if we tied them with ribbon?" I suggested. "We can bundle them together as they are in the chest. That might help her."

"I will fetch some ribbon."

Merytre brought several lengths of ribbon which I assumed she had cut from my gowns. We bundled up the packages and set them in the sack, careful to keep them in the same order as they were in the chest.

"Is that everything?" Merytre asked, as she tucked the last packets into the sack.

"If there is anything else that might be a potion ingredient, she has hidden it well." I cast my gaze around the chamber, but there was really nowhere else Ahmose might have stored more of the little linen packets.

"Surely she would have told Khaemmalu if anything was hidden, or at least hinted we would have to look hard," Merytre said. "She assumed we would find what she needed."

We took the sack back to Khaemmalu, who raised his eyebrows when he saw how full it was.

"Their method of return must be very complicated," he said.

"Thank you again. If there is ever a way I can return the favour, you only have to tell me.

"I am sure there will be something some day." He slung the sack over his shoulder. "Having someone in debt to you is never a bad thing."

CHAPTER 23

Since Ettu and Ahmose wouldn't try to return until after dark, I decided to pay a visit to Tiye. A maid I didn't recognise let me into her chamber and a quick glance around showed no sign of Nammu. Had she already fallen out of favour?

Tiye was standing at a window, watching something down on the ground, and looking very satisfied with herself.

"I suppose your bathing chamber has been newly cleaned this morning," I said.

No point pretending I was there for any other reason.

"Why, yes, it has." Tiye smirked at me over her shoulder. "Would you like to see?"

"Do you really need to make every new Ornament suffer like this?"

"It is how things have always been done. It was done to me and to every woman who followed me. Except for you, of course."

She turned to give me a pointed look.

"But Ishtar isn't an Ornament," I said. "Our father sent her here to serve me."

"And then Pharaoh noticed her. If he has decided she is an Ornament, who are we to argue with him?"

"Is that all there is to it? Pharaoh decides and a woman is now an Ornament?"

"Did you expect something else?" She raised her eyebrows at me. "Did you receive some special ceremony?"

"Of course not."

I had initially expected a marriage ceremony of some sort, but that seemed unlikely given the number of wives Pharaoh had. I sighed and tried to formulate a more persuasive argument.

"Tiye, why is it necessary to make the new women suffer? Think of the alliances you could build if you were kind to them. If you welcomed them in and helped them find their place here. They would respect you and appreciate your help."

"They would see me as soft and think they could replace me."

"Have I done that?"

She turned back from the window to eye me.

"It is early yet," she said. "You have only been here a few weeks."

"I have told you I don't want your position."

She gave me a look that said she didn't believe me.

"Even if it would mean you were next in line to be queen?" she asked.

"Why would that matter? Unless Isis dies, it is irrelevant who thinks they are waiting to take her place."

"She doesn't have to die." Tiye turned back to the window, her shoulders stiff now. "Pharaoh might decide to replace her. It has happened before."

"Isis replaced another queen?"

"I mean other pharaohs have replaced their queens." She spoke as if explaining to a rather dim child. "If it has happened once, it can happen again."

"Has Pharaoh ever given you any indication he might do such a thing?"

"If I can give him enough sons and he favours one of those over the sons Isis bears him, he might."

"I know you have six sons, but how many does she have?" Surely they were both past their childbearing years. However many they had now was likely as many as they would ever have.

"Only four. It seems the gods favour me more than her."

"And Pharaoh will decide which of them will be his heir?"

"He is very fond of my oldest." She smoothed her hand along the window sill. I couldn't tell whether she was checking for dust or if it was a way of controlling her emotions.

"So it is as simple as that? You give him a son he likes better than anyone else's and he will make you queen?"

Tiye sighed and turned back to face me.

"You are naive, Kassaya," she said. "That, I think, is what will be your downfall."

"I'm not trying to achieve anything."

"You should be." Her eyes narrowed and her gaze became a glare. "If you are to survive here, you should be doing everything in your power to catch Pharaoh's attention and bear him a child. That is the only way your future here is secure."

"What do you mean?"

She moved to the couch and took a long time to settle herself on it, smoothing her skirt over her knees before she spoke again.

"What do you think happens to the women who don't give him children?" she asked. "Do you think they get to stay here for the rest of their lives? Do you think this is some kind of retirement palace?"

"Of course not."

In truth, I hadn't thought about it and it was only now I realised I had seen few old women here who weren't servants. In fact, Tiye was the oldest Ornament I had met. I sat on the facing couch and made a show of smoothing my skirt the way she had.

"You will only be permitted to live here until your child-bearing years are ended," she said. "By then, you will either be retired to your own villa in the city, or returned to your father in disgrace."

"I could be sent home?" Hope flared within me. There was a way out of this place yet.

Tiye shook her head. "You don't want that. Aren't you here because your father made an alliance? Do you want to break that agreement by being returned to him?"

"Of course not."

"Then you need to start doing your duty. Get Pharaoh's attention."

"Why are you telling me these things? Doesn't every woman who gains his attention mean less attention for you?"

"I have given him sons." She looked at me evenly. "My future is assured, whether I am ever queen or not. You, however, have much work to do yet."

Did Tiye already anticipate the day she was granted her own villa? Yet she was determined to hold onto her power until the last moment.

"I came here expecting to be queen," I said. "I thought any

son I bore Pharaoh would be his heir. Did you think the same when you became an Ornament?"

"I already knew he had a queen and I knew he had sons. It was clear to me that the only way to control my future was to claim the Top position."

Of course, she had told me her mother was lady's maid to the queen. I hadn't thought to wonder how that came to be.

"Is your family Egyptian?" I asked.

Her features suggested otherwise, but I had never thought to ask before. There were many Ornaments here who were clearly not of Egyptian blood and I had become accustomed to seeing a variety of nationalities represented in their faces.

"My father is a minor royal. A cousin to Pharaoh, very distant. My mother's family was originally from Canaan. When they married, my father used his connection to Pharaoh to get her a position as lady's maid to the queen."

"You told me Pharaoh noticed you when you were a young child."

"I don't remember the first time I met him. I have been told I was no more than four years, but already Pharaoh thought I was beautiful. He said then he would make me an Ornament when I was older."

"You are fortunate you didn't have your imposingly beautiful sister with you when you met him."

She wouldn't miss the bitterness in my tone, but it was too late to take back the words.

Tiye actually chuckled. "I have to say, that was not a wise decision. Whatever possessed you to take her with you?"

I could hardly admit I had thought I would feel more confident knowing she was there with me. I wasn't even sure that was entirely the truth. Maybe I had wanted to impress on her that I was the Ornament, the one with status, and she was now merely a maid.

"She is my sister," I said. "I suppose I wanted to share the experience with her."

"Pharaoh has certainly made her feel welcome, from what I hear."

I hesitated, but I had to ask.

"Tiye, has Pharaoh ever…" My voice trailed away as I tried to find a way to put what I wanted to know into words.

"Ever what?" She gave me a sharp look and I was sure she knew what I was trying to ask.

"When Ishtar returned from her second night with him, she had… bruises around her neck."

"Kassaya." Tiye's tone was stiff now. "You must never forget Pharaoh is a living god. His word is law. Whatever he wants is his. There is nothing he can do to you that anyone will criticise him for, because Pharaoh *is* the law. Do you understand me?"

I thought I did. She was telling me not to ask questions. That it didn't matter what he had done to Ishtar, because he would do it again if he wanted to. And nobody would even try to stop him.

CHAPTER 24

The rest of the day passed with excruciating slowness. I knew it was too dangerous for Ettu and Ahmose to return until after dark, but I couldn't help wishing they would try. The only thing that made the wait bearable was the knowledge that Ettu was alive.

I fretted about how much Ahmose must be suffering with her broken wrist, but since I had sent all her herb packets with Khaemmalu, hopefully she could use something in the sack to ease her pain. When the servants brought our evening meal, I felt a surge of hope at this evidence of time passing. Surely they would return soon. I picked at some food, but was too nervous to eat.

They finally returned an hour after dark. I heard footsteps in the hallway and had the door open before Ettu had done any more than set her hand to the knob.

"Thank Marduk!" I said.

Ettu looked tired but otherwise well enough. It was Ahmose who worried me. Her face was white and her eyes shadowed. She seemed even more stooped than usual and her wig was slightly crooked, noticeable because the ends of her braids hung lower on one side. They had bandaged her wrist with strips torn from the bottom of Ettu's gown and Ahmose cradled her arm against her chest.

"Come, sit down," I said. "Merytre, fetch them something to drink. Are you hungry? Do you want bathing water?"

"Marduk, just let us sit first," Ettu said.

She helped Ahmose ease herself into the most comfortable chair, then fetched a couple of cushions to prop under her arm.

"Are you in very much pain?" I asked.

Ahmose shook her head, but I didn't miss the way she held her body very carefully, as if trying not to move her broken arm.

"It is not unbearable," she said. "There was willow bark in the sack you sent and I have chewed some of that. It is more effective as a tea, though."

"I will send for hot water." Merytre was already on her way out the door.

"She is in far more pain than she admits," Ettu said. "Without water, though, there was nothing we could do other than bandage her arm to stop the bones from rubbing against each other. I didn't dare leave her long enough to go looking for a well and we had no way to heat the water anyway."

"What happened?"

Ahmose was slumped back against the couch with her eyes closed. When she didn't reply, Ettu answered for her.

"She was barely out of sight of the Palace when she was set on by a man who decided he wanted her sack. When she refused to give it to him, he pushed her to the ground. She dropped the sack, and he grabbed it and ran away."

"I must have put out my arm to break my fall," Ahmose

said without opening her eyes. "My wrist broke as I landed. I heard a bone snap."

"What else can we do for you?" I asked. "Should I call for a healer?"

"No, no," Ahmose said. "There is nothing a healer will do for me that I can't do myself. I will feel much better once I have some willow bark tea. There are other things that will help too, but tomorrow will be soon enough to source them."

Had the man see her leave the Palace grounds? He might have thought it meant she could be carrying something valuable. There was no point asking Ahmose what she thought. If the man had seen her leave, there was nothing we could do about it now.

Merytre soon returned with a steaming jug. Ahmose instructed her on how to identify the willow bark within the linen packets in the sack. Merytre dropped a few pieces of bark into a mug and poured water over it.

"Let it steep for a few minutes," Ahmose said. "Do wake me if I fall asleep. I suddenly find myself very weary."

"It is probably the pain," Ettu said. "My sister broke her ankle as a child and I remember her being very tired afterwards. She did nothing but sleep for days."

I felt useless as I watched Merytre and Ettu fuss around Ahmose, bringing blankets and cushions, and making sure she was comfortable. My stomach growled and I hoped nobody else heard it. What would they think of me for being hungry at such a time?

"I have to say I am famished," Ettu said. "I haven't eaten since I left, other than a few dates Khaemmalu brought us."

"We should have sent something for you with Ahmose's sack." Why didn't I think of that? Of course they would be hungry. Ettu had been gone for two full nights.

I brought food for each of them, setting Ahmose's plate carefully on her lap. She gave me a wan smile, her eyes already drooping again.

I perched on the edge of a couch while Ettu ate, anxious to hear what news she brought, but not wanting to demand it from her before she had something in her belly. Ahmose sipped her tea, but ate no more than a nibble of bread.

"Half was able to get Lady Henutmire's letter to a courier," Ettu said at last. "He says there is still too much talk about Ishtar and how the queen is not happy with Pharaoh's fascination."

"He has made her an Ornament," I said. "She has her own chambers now."

"She has seen him again already?" Ettu asked. "A third time?"

"Not that I have heard, but of course I probably won't know if he calls for her again. I did tell her Half said she shouldn't go again too soon."

Ettu took a long drink, while I tried not to look impatient as I waited for the rest of her news.

"I suppose there is nothing we can do for her then," she said. "Tall is still acting odd. He definitely knows something, but he wouldn't tell me what."

"Has he told Half?"

"I couldn't ask in front of him, but I think Half would have said if he had."

"It must be difficult for him," I said. "Tall. Not being able to find the words he wants."

"Yes, but this is more than that. He isn't even trying to tell me."

"Perhaps somebody has threatened him," Merytre

suggested. "He might be too scared to tell you whatever he knows."

"Maybe," Ettu said with a frown.

"I should go to them," I said. "He might tell me."

"No," Ettu and Merytre said together.

"It is too dangerous," Ettu said.

"And your absence would be noticed," Merytre added. "Nobody would believe us if you weren't in your chambers and we claimed to not know where you were."

"You could say I have gone for a walk," I said. "Or that I went to visit someone but didn't tell you who."

"It is not a good idea," Ettu said. "I will go to them in a few days and ask again. I'm sure Tall will tell me what he knows eventually."

She rose to fill her plate a second time. "But tell me, what happened while we were gone?"

"Ishtar has asked for Belet-ili to be assigned to her," I said, watching Ettu's face carefully.

Ettu returned to her seat and took a large mouthful. She seemed to take a very long time to chew it.

"I see," she said at last. "I suppose Belet-ili is pleased about that."

"I haven't seen her since then."

Ettu took another mouthful and didn't seem inclined to comment any further.

"And what of you?" I had to know. "Would you prefer to serve Ishtar? I can ask for you to be reassigned to her, if you want."

"Of course not, my lady," Ettu said. "We have an agreement."

I had almost forgotten the pledge we made while we sailed from Babylon to Egypt. I had been thinking of Ettu as a friend, but she still saw me as nothing more than her mistress, and one who could eventually secure her future.

At the time I made our promise, I expected to be queen. I had thought I would have access to riches I could give Ettu to fund whatever life she desired. Now, I had nothing to pay her with but the jewels Father sent me here with, but I supposed that would be enough.

I mustn't forget again. It would be dangerous to forget that an alliance bought could just as easily become an alliance sold.

CHAPTER 25

Now I knew Ettu was safe, and we had done all we could for Ahmose's arm, I was able to reflect on Ineni's gathering. Henutmire's comment about talking business lingered in my mind and I asked Tiye what she meant the next time I went to visit her.

"You have yet to prove we can trust you." Her voice was lighter than I might have expected. "Surely you didn't expect us to share all our secrets with you immediately?"

"I suppose I didn't anticipate there were secrets to be shared," I said and immediately wished I hadn't. She had already called me naive. I didn't need to show her my inexperience yet again.

Tiye arched her eyebrows at me.

"Surely every group of women has their secrets," she said. "An outsider would need to prove herself before such things are revealed."

Gilukhipa had said something similar. I had almost forgotten.

"How would I prove myself?" I asked.

"You will know when the time comes."

Tiye changed the subject then and spoke of less weighty matters. Just as I was rising to take my leave, she mentioned the season was about to change.

"Already?" I asked, sitting back down again.

How long had I been here? The days all seemed the same to me: hot and dry with clear skies. It wasn't like Babylon, where increasingly humid days signalled the approach of the rainy season.

"*Shemu* is almost over," Tiye said. "And soon it will be *akhet*. The Great River will rise and break its banks. It will get hot very soon."

It had been *shemu* when I arrived. I hadn't been here as long as it felt.

"I thought it was already hot," I said. "But at least it will prove the year is passing. Every day here seems to feel the same as the one before."

"The changes are subtle. You will notice them more once you have been here longer. But for now, there is a ritual tonight to celebrate the change of season. You must come."

"What sort of ritual?"

"To honour Nephthys and Isis. Are you familiar with them?"

"I have heard of Isis." Ahmose had told us about her during our lessons on the ship. "She is a goddess and is married to Osiris, isn't she? He was killed by his brother and chopped into pieces."

"Yes, Isis searched the whole country until she found all his parts and she put him back together again. She resurrected him and bore him a son."

So even a goddess needed to produce sons.

"Nephthys is sister to Isis," Tiye said. "There is a chapel

behind the Palace. Any servant will be able to direct you. Be there at sunset, and come alone. Servants are not permitted to watch."

I agreed, then took my leave of her. Merytre was waiting for me at the end of Tiye's hallway.

"What do you know about a ritual celebration of the changing of the season?" I asked as we walked back to my chambers.

"There are many rituals through the year. We Egyptians will take any opportunity we can to celebrate."

"Apparently there is to be one tonight. What should I expect?"

"There will probably be music and singing. Possibly a reenactment of some story about a god, or more likely in this place, a goddess."

"Tiye mentioned Isis and Nephthys."

"Aah." She said nothing further as we walked.

"So what should I expect of a ritual celebrating those two goddesses?" I asked when she didn't offer anything else.

"Isis is a mother goddess. Fertility, protection, healing and the like. Nephthys is her opposite. Goddess of night, darkness and death."

"She sounds rather terrifying." And like something that would only give me more nightmares.

"They are both important goddesses. Life and death. Light and darkness. I expect your ritual will reflect those things."

The conversation left me with no clearer understanding, but it seemed that was all Merytre had to say on the matter. Maybe that was all she knew.

I left my chambers shortly before sunset with Ettu who would walk with me and wait outside the chapel, while Merytre stayed with Ahmose. I worried about Ettu waiting alone, but I also didn't want to leave Ahmose on her own. Now Ishtar had moved out, I really needed an additional lady's maid to sleep in my chambers.

"How well do you know my other maids?" I asked Ettu as we made our way through the Palace. "Is there one you think we can trust?"

"I have had little to do with them other than when they come to dress you in the mornings. Sehener always gives me a friendly smile, but the others mostly don't even look at me unless they need to speak to me. I think they are jealous I have a bedchamber in your suite."

"Surely I am not the only Ornament with lady's maids who stay with her? Tiye always has several maids there when I visit."

"It is very unusual for a maid to be given her own bedchamber as I have. From what I have heard, it is common for an Ornament to have at least one maid stay the night in case she is needed. But they sleep in a servant's chamber, which is available to whichever maid is there for the night, or they sleep on a couch. I don't think anyone other than Merytre and me have their own bedchambers, or even a shared one, on a permanent basis."

"I am sorry if that has caused problems for you," I said.

"Oh, no. I would much rather have my own bedchamber than sleep in the maids' dormitories. Besides, it is only your own lady's maids who have taken issue with it. Other servants don't care where I sleep."

"I don't suppose there is anything I can do to appease their jealousy?"

"It is not like you can give them all their own bedchambers, but I wonder if there might be something else you could do for them that would be special?"

"I could tell Panouk to move them into a dormitory of their own. One for only my maids. Would that help?"

"I was thinking something a little smaller. Like a picnic maybe."

"That is a good idea. We could have the kitchen provide a special meal for them. Lots of wine."

"Blankets on the grass," Ettu said. "Maybe late afternoon when it is a little cooler but before the insects come out. Shall I organise it?"

"Yes, let's do it tomorrow. Make arrangements with the kitchen — ask them for whatever you want — and make sure my maids realise this is just for them."

By now we had made our way through the Palace and out a back entrance. We followed a winding path that led between the trees until suddenly the chapel was in front of us. It stood in a clearing, a small mud brick building which could surely hold no more than a dozen people at once. The windows were shuttered and lamplight shone through the cracks. A handful of women waited nearby. Maids, by their gowns, which were not as fine as what an Ornament would wear. So, despite Tiye's instruction to come alone, I wasn't the only woman who had brought an escort.

"I will wait with them," Ettu said with a nod towards the maids, and left me to approach the chapel on my own.

My heart pounded as I walked the last stretch of the path. Why was I suddenly so nervous? I had attended many religious rituals in Babylon. This one could hardly be much different. But I didn't know who else would be there and the women from Ineni's gathering had made it clear they didn't yet trust me. Would this be another group of women whose confidence I would have to win?

CHAPTER 26

The door opened as I reached the chapel. Silhouetted against the light was a woman with the head of a cat. Startled, I stepped back and almost tripped.

"Greetings," the cat-headed woman said.

She held something out to me. I turned it over and a pair of empty eye sockets stared up at me.

"What is this?" I asked.

"Put it over your face."

A mask then, like hers. It was light, made of papyrus maybe.

"Do I know you?" I asked as I positioned the mask over my face and tied the ribbon behind my head.

"Do not speak."

As soon as my mask was in place, she gestured for me to follow her. Inside, candlelight revealed half a dozen women standing in a circle. The cat-headed woman led me to them and pointed to the spot where I was to stand. I studied the women, wondering if I knew any of them.

One wore a mask of a cow's head. Another, a beast I

thought might be a crocodile, like those I had glimpsed on our journey down the Great River. There was a mask that might have been the head of a beetle and one that was a fearsome creature I couldn't identify. From the way that woman held herself, I thought she might be Tiye. I didn't recognise the creatures depicted by the masks of the other women. What was mine supposed to be? I hadn't seen it well enough to guess and I didn't dare take it off now to look.

I felt rather awkward as we stood there silently. Were we waiting for others to join us, or merely for the ritual to begin? My question was answered when the cat-headed woman joined the circle, now bearing a large goblet. As she offered it to the woman on her left, the one with the head of a cow, a single drum began a slow, steady beat. The cow-headed woman raised her mask just high enough to take a sip from the goblet, then passed it to the woman on her left. The goblet went around the circle until it reached me.

It was made of smokey grey glass, smooth under my fingers and warm from the hands it had already passed through. Like the others before me, I took a sip. The liquid was odd-tasting, bitter and herby, although sweetened some-what with honey. I passed the goblet to the woman beside me. At last, it reached the cat-headed woman again. I expected her to set it down, but she took another sip and passed it on again. The drum continued to beat.

Three times I drank from the goblet before the cat-headed woman finally placed it on the floor. She held out her hands to the women on either side of her. I clasped the hands of those beside me and waited, my heart pounding harder now. My head was starting to swim.

A delicate tune began, played on a harp very softly at first and then louder. Beneath it, the steady beat of the drum continued. I hadn't seen any musicians when I entered the room, but then my focus had been on the women in the circle. Perhaps they were in an adjoining chamber.

Around the outside of the circle, a figure moved. As she passed behind the women across from me, I saw her back was hunched and she grasped her head as if it hurt. Her mask seemed to be that of a lion or, I supposed, a lioness. Round and round she went, her feet moving in time with the sounds of the harp.

The harp played on and the lion-woman continued to circle us. My head swam and the chamber seemed to tilt on its side. The lioness grew larger until she was twice the size she had been before. She raised a paw and raked sharp claws through the air. When she caught me looking, she growled, low and menacing. I wanted to look away, but my gaze seemed locked on the lioness.

At some point I realised another musician had joined the harpist and the drummer. The jangle of a tambourine that seemed to play a different tune altogether. As the harpist and tambourinist competed, the drum continued its steady beat. The music swelled and the cacophony filled my ears until I couldn't even think. I could only watch and listen. The lioness continued to prowl around our circle. The drum went on and on.

Dread welled within me. The lioness was looking for a victim. Seeking weakness. What clue would tell her that one woman was weaker than the others? Was it me? Would the lioness eat me?

My body felt both light and heavy at the same time. My legs could barely hold me up, but the only thing stopping me from floating away into the air was the hands of the women on either side of me. No, they weren't women. They were beasts of some kind, but I hadn't seen their faces clearly enough to tell. Was I even a woman anymore, or had I too turned into some unknowable beast?

Round and round the lioness went. The music crashed and clashed, seemingly following no tune anymore, just a discordant series of notes, while the drum continued its steady pace. I floated off the floor, but the beasts on either side of me held me down. Two more women entered the circle and came to stand in the centre, although I didn't see where they came from or how they passed between the beasts with joined hands.

They wore flowing golden gowns and long wings extended from their shoulders. The tips of the feathers brushed the floor as they walked. One wore a headdress that seemed to be a chair. No, maybe it was a throne. My thoughts were muddy and it took me a while to remember the name of the goddess who wore a throne on her head. Isis. The other had a pair of horns with a sun nestled between them. She must be Nephthys.

Isis and Nephthys danced, even though the jarring music seemed to provide no rhythm for them to move to. They danced together and then they broke free of the circle of beasts and joined the lioness that prowled behind us. The lioness pursued the goddesses, or maybe they pursued her. Round and round. The drum pounded, louder, faster. My heart beat in time with it.

Then Nephthys was on the floor, writhing, dying. Isis and the lioness continued pacing around the circle. The harp and the tambourine faded away and the only sounds were the steady beat of the drum and the footsteps of Isis and the lioness.

After an age, Nephthys twitched. Slowly, so slowly, she

rose and joined Isis and the lioness circling us. The drum faded. Nephthys and Isis were gone and the lioness alone traced the perimeter of our circle. Then she too slipped away. The drum stopped. We were no longer beasts. We were women again.

The women on either side of me released my hands. My palms were sweaty and my heart beat too fast. I waited for someone to speak, to explain what had happened, but nobody did. One by one, the women left.

CHAPTER 27

"Well," Ettu said as we headed back into the Palace. "What happened? I heard music."

"It was… strange. I'm not sure what I expected, but it wasn't that."

She walked in silence while I sorted through my thoughts.

"Everyone wore masks," I said eventually. "Strange masks like the heads of animals."

"Like goddesses?"

"I suppose. We shared a drink. It must have been hallucinogenic, because things got very weird after that. We stood in a circle and held hands, and a woman with the head of a lion danced around us." I felt rather daft as I tried to explain the ritual. My words didn't convey how menacing it had felt, but I didn't know how else to describe it. "There were two women who I think were supposed to be Isis and Nephthys."

"Priestesses?" Ettu asked. "Or Ornaments."

"I didn't recognise them. They danced around us with the lion-woman and I think Nephthys died. Then she came back to life and it was all over."

"The music sounded fierce."

"It was a strange experience. It felt… threatening. Dangerous, somehow."

"Dangerous for you?"

I could feel her studying me as we walked.

"I don't know. It was just strange and my thoughts are all confused."

"Whatever it was you drank probably made everything seem very unreal."

"I'm not even sure now how much of it really happened. Like the lioness. At one time, she was twice as big as me."

"That can't be real. It must have been the drink."

"I suppose."

But Ettu hadn't seen what I had. Was it really because of what we drank, or had something unexplainable happened in the chapel?

Fatigue washed over me as we made our way through the Palace and by the time we reached my chambers, I yawned so hard that tears ran down my cheeks. I could barely keep awake long enough to undress and set my wig on a shelf.

Then I was walking alone through the Palace gardens. I became aware that someone, or something, kept pace with me behind a row of shrubs. I peered between the shrubs, but couldn't make out who it was.

"Hello?" I called. "Is someone there?"

A low growl greeted my words.

My heart pounded and I quickened my pace.

A lion sprang out from behind the shrubs and landed ahead of me on the path. We eyed each other and it snarled, lifting its lips to reveal long, yellowed teeth.

I turned back the way I had come and then it was there

too. When I turned around, it was still behind me. There were two lions.

As I ran, they sprinted in circles around me.

"No," I cried out. "Leave me alone. I didn't see anything."

The lions flung themselves at me, grabbing me by the shoulders and shaking me so hard my teeth slammed together.

"My lady," they growled.

I woke to Ettu shaking my shoulders.

"My lady," she said. "Wake up. It is just a dream."

My breath caught in my throat and for a moment I couldn't remember how to breathe. My heart pounded as loud as the drums during the ritual.

"Are you awake?" Ettu asked.

I sat up. My whole body was damp with sweat and my hands trembled. I took a deep breath, trying to steady myself.

"Yes," I said. "I had a terrible dream."

"A nightmare, more like," Merytre said, peering over Ettu's shoulder. "It is hardly surprising after that ritual. Ettu told me about it."

"Lions were chasing me through the gardens," I said.

"There are definitely no lions in the gardens." Ettu retrieved my blanket from the floor and spread it back over my bed. "Are you all right now?"

"Yes, go back to sleep."

They left and I lay back down. It was just a dream, I told myself. There are no lions here, either in the gardens or in my bedchamber. But my heartbeat was still unsteady and I couldn't bring myself to close my eyes. I rose and lit the lamp. I got back into bed, comforted by the cheery glow, although it was a long time before I slept again.

I was the last to rise in the morning, having slept right

through dawn and the bird's morning song. In the sitting chamber, Ettu and Merytre were standing together at the window, while Ahmose sat on a couch, her arm propped up on cushions.

"Did you go back to sleep after your nightmare?" Ettu asked me.

"I did eventually," I said. "What are you looking at?"

"Just watching Sutem make his way around the grounds," Merytre said, shooting me a grin. "It makes for a rather pleasant view."

"Your lady's maids arrived some time ago," Ettu said. "I told them you were already dressed and sent them on their way."

It would be a relief to not have to endure their attentions today. I would never get used to sitting naked on the stool in my bathing chamber while a team of women worked on me.

"How is your arm?" I asked Ahmose as I poured myself some melon juice. "Do you want any of this?"

Ahmose shook her head. "It hurts, but the willow bark helps."

I finished my juice and made my way around the chamber, sitting in various chairs before deciding they weren't what I was looking for. The terror of my nightmare still loomed close and I couldn't quite shake off the horror of the circling lions. Maybe a walk would help. Surely being out in the sunlight would dispel my fears. Ettu came with me, but being in the same gardens I had dreamed of only made me feel worse. My dream still felt far too close and the possibility of a lion hiding behind each patch of shrubbery made me uneasy.

I was about to tell Ettu we should return to my chambers, when we rounded a bend in the path and encountered a woman crouched beside a flower bed. A linen shawl covered her head and hid her face from our view. A servant maybe, for she wasn't dressed like an Ornament. She seemed to be whispering to the flowers. I averted my eyes and made to hurry past her. Perhaps she was an elderly servant who had lost her mind.

As we drew near her, the woman looked up. The shawl fell back, revealing her face was covered in what seemed to be scales. Ettu gasped and I barely restrained my own exclamation.

"Why are you here?" the woman asked.

Her stare felt like it pierced right through me.

"We were taking a walk," I said, pleased my voice didn't reveal my discomfort at her appearance. "I'm sorry if we disturbed you."

"You shouldn't be here," she said. "This is not a place for the likes of you."

"What do you mean?"

"They will draw you in. You should leave while you can. You do not want to be involved with what is coming."

"What is it that is coming?" I asked.

"Leave. It is not too late."

She rose slowly as if her joints pained her, and hurried away.

"Wait," I called after her. "I don't understand."

She disappeared behind a stand of dom palms.

"Come on," I said to Ettu. "I have to find her."

But by the time we reached the dom palms, there was no sign of the woman.

"Where did she go?" I asked.

There were too many directions she could have fled in. Too many trees and bushes that might shield her from my view if she was still here.

"That was unsettling," Ettu said. "I feel quite disturbed."

"Who was she? I have never seen her before."

"Neither have I. I would have remembered her face. Did you see the scales?"

"I have never seen someone who looked like that before."

I took one last look around, then turned back towards the path.

"Should we report her to someone?" Ettu asked.

"For what? Walking in the gardens?"

"Well," she floundered. "Surely she wasn't meant to be here."

"She must be. How could she get in otherwise? She must live in the Palace."

"Wouldn't we have heard about a woman with a face of scales?"

"There are thousands of women here. She can't be the only one who looks..." My voice trailed away as I searched for a description that sounded kinder than what I had almost said.

"I suppose she mightn't be all that different from Half." Ettu's voice was tentative, as if she was reconsidering her point of view, but wasn't yet sure of it. "People judge him for his looks, but he is no less intelligent than any other man I have met. Maybe it is the same for her? Certainly her speech didn't suggest there was anything wrong with her brain."

It made me feel ashamed of my own reaction to the woman. Although I watched for her as we returned to my chambers, I saw no further sign of her.

CHAPTER 28

*B*ack in my chambers, it was a relief to occupy my mind with Ettu's plans for the picnic, rather than dwelling on my nightmare. She told me about the food she had ordered, watching my face anxiously as if expecting me to disagree or say it was too much. I only listened and nodded. After all, I had told her to request whatever she wanted.

Around midafternoon, Ettu said it was time to leave for the picnic. She gave me what seemed to be a significant look, clearly waiting for something. Merytre was already at the door, barely restraining her excitement.

"Go on then." I looked up from the needlework I was pretending to work on, although I had spent more time unpicking it than stitching. "You don't want to be late."

"You are coming, aren't you?" Ettu asked.

"Me? Oh no, I will stay here with Ahmose."

"But…" Ettu's voice trailed off. She glanced at Merytre as if asking for her help.

"Is there a problem?" I asked.

"Well, my lady, we thought you would be there too," Merytre said.

"At the picnic? They wouldn't want me there. This was supposed to be a treat for my maids."

I set the needlework aside with a sigh. There was really no point. I would never be able to stitch neatly enough, no matter how much I tried.

"But part of the treat was for them to spend time with you," Merytre said. "They are very excited about it."

"I'm sorry," Ettu said. "I think I misunderstood. I told them all you would be there. Never mind. I will just explain I was wrong."

"No, no." I got to my feet and maybe not as unwillingly as they seemed to expect. "If you have already said I will go, I don't want to disappoint them. This was supposed to be a treat, after all. I just didn't think anyone would want me there."

"Why ever not?" Ettu asked. "Of course they want you to go."

"I didn't think they would want their mistress there with them."

"They have probably spent all day telling anyone who will listen they're going to a picnic with you," Merytre said.

"When I told them, the first thing anyone asked was whether you were going," Ettu added.

"I'm hardly going to disappoint them then," I said. "Ahmose, did you want to come?"

"I'm actually feeling rather weary," Ahmose said. She was ensconced in a chair with her arm propped up on cushions and looked quite comfortable even if she was still somewhat pale. "Unless you have need of me, I will stay here."

"Of course," I said. "Make sure you bar the door behind us, though."

"We will bring you back a treat," Ettu said. "I asked the kitchen to make some special pastries. Perhaps one of those?"

Ahmose nodded, but seemed unable to muster up a smile. Perhaps she was still in more pain than she admitted. A broken arm must be hard on such an old woman.

Ettu and Merytre chattered as we made our way out to the gardens. They led me to a pretty grove where covered platters were spread over a blanket on the grass. The serving woman who had been left to keep watch over it disappeared as soon as we arrived.

"We are a little early," Ettu said. "They will be here shortly, but I wanted to make sure everything was in order before they came."

She inspected the food, lifting each cover to peer beneath it. From the way she nodded and muttered to herself, I gathered everything was as she expected. The women arrived in groups of twos and threes, and I made an effort to learn their names. Their excited faces and sparkling eyes made me feel rather bad I hadn't done so earlier.

Khensa and Hemetre were the first to arrive, followed by Sehener, Nebatah and Mutnofret. Ipu came with Tuya, whose face I didn't recognise. Apparently she had been appointed to me only that morning to replace Nammu. With Ettu and Merytre, all nine of my current maids were accounted for. Belet-ili hadn't yet been replaced and I wondered whether she would be. Surely nine lady's maids was plenty for anyone.

The women were quick to fill their plates and find places to sit. There was a fine assortment of food, with whole baked fish, chickpeas mashed with garlic, a salad of crunchy onions and cucumber, bowls of olives and dom palm nuts, and sliced watermelon. As a special treat, Ettu had arranged for little pastries sweetened with honey and dates.

"This is a very fine feast, my lady," one of the women said to me.

I studied her face, trying to remember her name. She had been one of the first to arrive, Khensa or Hemetre, although I couldn't remember now which was which. They both had round faces and short wigs.

"It is Ettu you should thank," I said. "She made all the arrangements."

"Oh, but only because you told me to," Ettu said quickly. "It was so thoughtful of you to suggest a picnic."

She clearly didn't want the women to know it had been her idea. I only nodded, not knowing what else to say.

"So Belet-ili has been reassigned," one of the women said. Was she Sehener? Her face was long and narrow, with high eyebrows. I tried to fix her name in my mind.

"Yes, she has gone to Lady Ishtar," another replied. Mutnofret maybe. Her wig was like Merytre's, with the front section brushed forward and pinned with a pretty clasp.

"Is Nammu still with Lady Tiye?" Sehener asked.

Silence greeted her question and I realised most of the women were either looking at me or very studiously looking elsewhere. Maybe they weren't sure whether they should talk about Nammu in front of me.

"As far as I know, she is," I said with what I hoped was a friendly smile.

"My lady, the most awful gossip has been spread about you," Sehener said, obviously taking my smile as permission to continue.

Someone shushed her, but she waved away their objection.

"No, she should know," she said.

"What kind of gossip?" I asked.

"That you stole jewels from Lady Tiye and were almost thrown out of the Palace for it."

"I heard you were arrested," Hemetre said. Maybe she felt bolder now since I hadn't chastised Sehener.

"And that you went before a magistrate who said you were guilty but released you on Pharaoh's order," Ipu added.

"What a load of nonsense," Ettu said. "Do any of you really believe such rubbish? You are all old enough to know there is little truth to most of the gossip you hear in this place."

"Then tell us what really happened," Sehener said. "If we knew the truth, we could correct people when they speak about it."

"Yes," Ipu said. "We would be happy to make sure folk know the truth, especially if it presents my lady in a more favourable light."

"You only have to tell us what you want them to know and we will be sure to tell everyone," Khensa said.

I glanced at Ettu, wondering what she thought, but she only shrugged at me.

"Nammu stole the jewels herself," I said. "She planted them in my chambers and then told the administrator I was the thief."

The women's exclamations drowned out anything else I might have said. I figured that was enough anyway. If they spread that news, it would destroy Nammu's reputation and hopefully restore mine. It mightn't be much of a punishment for her, but it was something.

"Nammu told me you never liked her," Mutnofret said. "That when you learned you were to be sent to Egypt, you asked for her by name, although she didn't know what she ever did to you. Is that true?"

I was so surprised that it took me a moment too long to answer.

"She told me the same thing," Sehener said.

"And that you said you would ensure she never returned to Babylon for as long as you lived," Hemetre added.

"She told me you came to Egypt thinking you would be queen," Khensa said.

"All lies," I managed finally. There was only one thing they said that was true, but they didn't need to know that. "My father, the king of Babylon, made the decision. It was he who decided Nammu, Belet-ili and Ettu would accompany me."

Ettu skilfully turned the conversation to other Palace gossip, leaving me free to fume about Nammu's lies. I hadn't realised the depth of her enmity towards me. Did she truly not understand I was just as much a victim of my father's decision as she was? I had thought her theft of Tiye's jewels was intended as retribution for not being given her own bedchamber, but maybe that was merely the last bitter blow for her. She must have already been harbouring resentment about being separated from Ishtar and sent away from Babylon.

We stayed out in the garden until the sun started to set and the biting insects descended. As they rose to leave, each of my maids thanked me nicely for inviting them to the picnic. I smiled and nodded and tried not to show that already I wasn't quite sure which name went with which face. Sehener was the only one I definitely remembered. Her narrow face was distinctive and I recognised her name after Ettu had said she was the only maid who was friendly towards her.

"Well, that was a success," Ettu said as we returned to my chambers.

"Do you think they enjoyed it?" I asked.

"They thought it was wonderful," she said. "You certainly gave them reason to be loyal to you."

"The food was very good," Merytre said. "It was far finer than they would normally get and they ate every last one of those pastries."

"Except for the two I hid away for Ahmose." Ettu tapped the linen-covered plate she carried. "It was fortunate I grabbed them before they all arrived or she would have missed out."

They continued to chatter, but I stopped listening, busying myself instead with musing about my lady's maids. Although I had found allies here, more would always be valuable. Did any of those women have the potential to be allies?

CHAPTER 29

"I met a strange woman in the gardens recently," I said to Tiye when I next visited her a day or two after the picnic.

"Oh?" She arched her eyebrows at me as if anticipating an amusing story.

"She had scales all over her face."

"Oh, her." She waved her hand at me dismissively. "She's a priestess. Very highly regarded when she was younger."

A priestess? That was the last thing I expected. Tiye gave me a curious look when I didn't reply.

"Did she say something odd?" she asked. "She has a reputation as something of a seer, but she can be unreliable."

"A seer?" Did that mean her words to me were a prophecy?

"What did she say?" Tiye asked.

They will draw you in. You should leave while you can. You do not want to be involved with what is coming.

"Nothing much," I said. "I hardly remember it now."

I felt a twinge of guilt about lying to her, but if there was some kind of plot afoot, I had no doubt Tiye was part of it.

"Were you at the ritual the other night?" I asked, determined to change the subject.

"The women who attend such things wear masks for a reason. If you attended, you would be wise to keep it to yourself."

"I didn't say I went. Besides, you invited me, so I assume you intended going yourself."

Tiye gave me a sharp look. "You need to learn how to control your face. I suspect you don't realise how much it gives away."

"What is wrong with my face?"

"Nothing. You just need to work on hiding your feelings. I can always tell from your face when you're lying."

"I don't lie, not often anyway, and if I do, there's a good reason for it."

"That may be, but if you lie to someone, you don't want them to know. Your face reveals quite clearly when what you say isn't what you believe."

I rose and went to the window, searching the gardens for any sign of the scaled woman as I tried to find a reply.

"I'm not good at things like this," I said finally. "Politics. Intrigue."

"If you are to survive here, you need to learn to be good at them."

"What if I don't want to? What if I just want to bear sons for Pharaoh like my father told me to and live my life away from people staring at me."

"I thought you were smarter than that."

I turned back to her. "What do you mean?"

"You haven't always gone about things the way I would have, but since you arrived, you have shown yourself to be reasonably intelligent. You've made some good moves. Found some allies. I had come to believe you had some ambition. Now you say all you want is to have sons and avoid being stared at?"

"It's easy for you to say. You have already given Pharaoh sons. I'm supposed to be strengthening the alliance between Babylon and Egypt, but I have barely had a chance to say two words to Pharaoh, let alone—"

I stopped abruptly, uncomfortable about discussing such a thing with Tiye who clearly had far more experience than me in such matters.

"And yet your sister has already spent the night with him twice." Her voice was cool, even if her face hid her emotions far better than mine apparently did.

"You lecture me about what my face reveals, but your voice tells me what you think about Ishtar," I said.

Tiye gave me a haughty look.

"I suppose she is still cleaning your bathing chamber every morning?" I asked. "I haven't heard any gossip about her being found escaping out a window."

Tiye scoffed. "No, your sister is not the type to do that. She scrubs my chamber like a dutiful little Ornament. Doesn't do a particularly good job of it, but she is obedient. Unlike someone else I know."

"And yet it was me who was sent here, and not her," I said, and immediately wished I hadn't. My voice betrayed my bitterness, even if I had managed to keep it from my face.

"Yes, we have all wondered about that. Both you and she have been tightlipped on why it was not the elder who was sent."

I turned back to the window before my face could give me away.

"I can't imagine your father chose to send the younger

sister if the elder was available," she said. "So I'm guessing she was either already promised to someone or she was with child."

Thank Marduk she couldn't see my face. When I didn't reply, Tiye chuckled.

"It's all right, Kassaya. You can keep your secret — for now. We will find out eventually."

"There's nothing much to tell," I said. "Our father made the decision and he chose to send me. He is my king and it is not my place to question him."

"I suspect there is more to the story than you say. But that will do for now."

I made sure my face was calm before I returned to the couch.

"I meant to ask," I said. "Does Nammu still serve you? I haven't seen her the last couple of times I have been here."

"She does, although I can't bear to have her near me for long. I don't mind a bit of gossip, but she's a nasty one. Takes too much pleasure in relating any unfortunate news. I have had her assigned to laundry when I have no need of her, which fortunately is most of the time."

Tiye was a strange contradiction. She freely confessed to having engineered the death of the woman whose position she wanted, and yet she objected to malicious gossip. I wasn't sure I would ever understand her.

CHAPTER 30

After my visit with Tiye, Ettu and I returned to my chambers. I hadn't even put my hand to the knob before the door was flung open. Merytre stood there, her face flushed and her eyes wild.

"Merytre!" I said. "Whatever has happened."

"I think we should go inside first," Ettu murmured to me. "Whatever it is, I doubt we want to be discussing it in the hallway."

"The most marvellous thing, my lady," Merytre said the moment the door was closed. "A messenger boy came. Pharaoh is visiting tomorrow and has asked for you."

"Me?" I could hardly believe it. After the disaster that was my first meeting with him, I had wondered whether he would ever call for me again.

"He plans to spend the afternoon sailing on the pleasure lake behind the Palace and he has asked for you to join him."

"How wonderful," Ettu said. "You will finally have a chance to impress him. I have no doubt that once he spends some time with you, he will be very interested."

"I don't think Pharaoh is the type of man who values a woman like me," I said.

Ettu stammered.

"I'm sorry," I said. "I know you were trying to make the best of the situation."

"Yes," she said, a little indignantly. "If Pharaoh cannot see what a worthy addition you make to his Ornaments, he is a fool."

"Hush," Merytre said. "You don't want to say something like that too loudly. You never know who might be passing in the hallway to overhear."

Ettu pursed her lips and seemed to refrain from saying anything further only with great effort.

"If he plans to sail all afternoon, whatever will I talk to him about for so long?" I asked.

I flung myself onto a couch, already too anxious about the outing to take any satisfaction in the invitation.

"He likes to talk about himself from what I hear," Merytre said. "As long as you can keep the focus on him, I doubt you will have to say much about anything."

"But how do I do that? Do I ask him questions? I wouldn't even know where to start."

My education, thorough as it was due to my own interests, had been lacking in how to talk to a man. Ishtar would fare much better in such a thing than me. She had spent her formative years practising her wit and charm on any man she could.

"What kind of things can you talk knowledgeably about if he wants you to make conversation?" Ettu asked.

"Babylonian politics," I said. "And a little of world politics. Geography, history, art. I can talk about music, although I never learned to play an instrument. Philosophy, reason, and—"

Ettu and Merytre were both shaking their heads.

"Those are all excellent topics," I said. "They show I have an educated mind."

"Pharaoh is not interested in your brain, my lady," Merytre said.

"We should think a little more simply," Ettu said. "You could ask him what his favourite food is."

"Whether he likes to hunt," Merytre said.

"Oh, that's a good one," Ettu said. "You could ask him about the fiercest animal he has ever killed."

"Whether he likes chariots and if he goes out riding in them."

"And if he hunts from them."

"Which god he favours."

"Whether there is a particular celebration that is his favourite."

"What kind of wine he drinks."

"What his bedchamber looks like," Ettu said.

"Yes, that's excellent," Merytre said. "You should ask a lot of other questions first, but then you could lead him into thinking about his bedchamber and it might put him in mind of how he hasn't bedded you yet."

"Merytre!" My cheeks heated as reliably as ever.

"That is why you are here, is it not?" she asked. "There is no point pretending you have any other purpose, not with us."

"We are only trying to help," Ettu said.

"So, basically, I should ask him a lot of very simple questions about himself and what he likes," I said. "Is that what you are saying?"

"I know that doesn't sound terribly interesting," Ettu said.

"No, it doesn't."

It sounded like our sailing expedition would be not unlike when Pharaoh called us all together in the courtyard to spend hours telling us how everything good in the world happened because of him. I doubted he would need much encouragement to talk about himself all afternoon.

"Isn't there something else we could discuss?" I asked. "Something that would prompt a genuine conversation?"

Ettu and Merytre looked at each other.

"She could—" Ettu started.

"Maybe—" Merytre said at the same time.

"Perhaps he will surprise you, my lady," Ettu said, with renewed enthusiasm. "You just need to figure out what he is interested in and then you'll be able to have a conversation with him."

"His family history, maybe," Merytre said.

"What do you know about that?" I asked. "I don't even know who his father was."

"His name was Setnakhte," Merytre said. "And his mother's name was..." She paused to think. "Tiye-Merenaset, I think."

"Tiye?" I asked.

"It's a common name," she said. "Now let me think. I'm sure I know more than that. Setnakhte was very old when he became Pharaoh. He wasn't Egyptian born. Syrian, I think. And he was only Pharaoh for a couple of years."

"What happened to him?"

She shook her head. "I don't recall. This was well before I was born, you understand. I only know what I have heard. Folk don't talk much about him. I think he didn't rule long enough for people to develop any feelings about him, good or bad. Since he was so old, he had Pharaoh — Ramses, that is — act for him in most matters. So when Setnakhte went to the

West and Ramses took the throne, there wasn't much change. Everything just went on as it had because he had mostly already been doing it all anyway."

"Is that his name? Ramses?"

How strange to realise I'd never heard his name before. I'd only ever heard him called Pharaoh. It seemed obvious now, but I hadn't even realised he had another name. Tiye had mentioned somebody named Ramses, but I couldn't remember whether it was her son or that of Isis. He must have been named for Pharaoh.

"Ramses the Third, I believe," Merytre said. "He probably had a different name before he took the throne, but I don't think I have ever heard it. He is named in honour of one of his ancestors, Ramses the Second. He was very famous."

"I have never heard of him." I prided myself on my education, so how was it I didn't know of such a famous ancestor of the man who ruled the country which was our biggest ally?

"Ramses the Second singlehandedly defeated the Hittite army in battle," Merytre said. "And he was responsible for taking the city of Kadesh from them."

"Singlehandedly?" I asked. "You mean one man defeated a whole army?"

"That is the way I learned it," Merytre said. "I admit, it sounds rather…"

"Far fetched," Ettu said.

"Impressive," Merytre said, "but that is how it is told."

"I suppose I could ask Pharaoh about that," I said.

"I'm sure he would be most happy to tell you," Ettu said. "I think if you can get him talking about just one topic he is interested in, you won't have to do much after that."

CHAPTER 31

As the time for my outing with Pharaoh drew closer, I became increasingly nervous.

"Perhaps you would care to try some needlework?" Ettu asked, eyeing me as I paced around the sitting chamber. "You have hardly done anything on that piece you started."

She was comfortably seated on a couch by a window and seemed content to be embroidering a strip of linen to re-hem the gown she ruined to bandage Ahmose's broken arm. I had said she should throw the gown out, but she and Merytre both insisted it could be saved. I waved away her suggestion.

"I would rather not subject a perfectly fine piece of linen to my poor needlework ability," I said, pausing briefly at the window.

On the far side of the grounds, a figure made its way along the length of the wall. I watched for a while, trying to make out who it was. It wasn't likely to be Khaemmalu, although I found myself hoping it might be. More likely, it was Sutem or one of the other day guards. I hadn't spoken to Khaemmalu since he helped Ettu and Ahmose get back into the grounds.

He probably still wanted answers that I didn't know how to give him.

Merytre was also stitching, although her piece was far more ambitious than Ettu's: a wall hanging for her bedchamber depicting a woman with the head of a lion. I supposed she was meant to be a goddess, although I didn't ask which one. In truth, I tried not to look at it, because it reminded me uncomfortably of my nightmares about being stalked in the gardens.

I was the only one doing nothing and I felt lazy, but I couldn't focus my mind on anything. Even Ahmose was busy, although her broken arm meant nobody offered her any stitching. When Merytre had asked what she was doing, Ahmose said she was compiling a list of the herbs she needed to replace the ones that were in her stolen sack. She rattled off a number of them and I couldn't imagine how she kept such a lengthy list in her head. Surely Ahmose had to be one of the cleverest women I had ever met.

So although she looked like she was merely sitting on the couch and staring at nothing, she was just as busy as Ettu and Ahmose. I hadn't forgotten I needed to convince her to show me how to make her potion, but I thought I should wait until her arm was less painful.

My entire team of lady's maids arrived to prepare me for the outing with Pharaoh. Belet-ili had been replaced with a girl of about ten years whose black skin marked her as a foreigner. She hung back as they bathed me and seemed unsure what she was supposed to do. I was pleased to see Merytre notice her uncertainty and give her a couple of small tasks.

It wasn't until I was sitting on a stool in my bedchamber with the women trying various wigs on my head and arguing about which was the most suitable, that I had a chance to speak to the girl. I gestured for her to come closer, noting again how she stood a little apart from the others.

"What is your name?" I asked.

"Abar, my lady," she said, her voice so low I could barely hear her. She spoke hesitantly, as if unconfident with the Egyptian language.

"Is this your first placement in the Palace?"

"Yes, my lady."

I waited, expecting her to offer more information, but she only looked at the floor and said nothing.

"How did you come to work here?" I asked.

She met my eyes then and I was taken aback by the hatred in them.

"I was stolen from my country," she said. "Soldiers of your Pharaoh came to fight the men of my land. They killed all our men and stole women and girls. My sister and I were taken."

I hardly knew how to respond. Was an apology appropriate? Sympathy?

"What is your country?" I asked and immediately knew I had said the wrong thing. I should have offered something sympathetic first.

"Kush."

From the way she straightened her shoulders and raised her head as she spoke, I could tell how proud she was of her homeland. Maybe she, like me, had someone else's voice in her head in a moment like that. *Show Pharaoh what the women of Babylon are made of.*

"I am sorry you were taken from there," I said.

"Sorry enough to have me sent home?" she asked.

Her eyes blazed defiance. This was not a girl suited for a position as a maid. There was no obedience in her. No humility or willingness to serve. She was angry and she wanted me to know it.

"I wish I could, but I don't have that sort of power."

"You are one of the wives of the king here, are you not? You can tell him to send me home. Me and my sister."

"Where is she?" I asked.

"I don't know. She was taken somewhere else and nobody has told me anything."

"Ettu," I said. "Would you ask around and see if you can find out where Abar's sister is?"

"Her name is Atahar," Abar said.

Ettu set her hand on the girl's shoulder.

"I will do my best to find word of her," she said.

"And you will tell me what you learn?" Abar asked. "No matter what it is?"

"Of course," Ettu said. "She is your sister."

Abar seemed satisfied with Ettu's promise and I was once again free to turn my mind to worrying about making conversation with Pharaoh.

My maids finally left, although not before they offered many good wishes for the afternoon. There were a lot of giggles and comments whispered behind upraised hands, and I suspected those remarks were more lewd than what they said to my face.

Ettu and Merytre escorted me to the lake. I didn't like Ahmose staying alone, but it wouldn't be fair to ask her to walk so far. I told her to bar the door behind us and to not open it until we returned.

Ettu and Merytre were silent as we walked through the palace. The hallways seemed busier than ever and the noise of people walking and chattering, doors opening and closing, and folk going about their business meant I could hardly hear myself think. I tried to breathe slowly to settle both my mind and my racing heart, but it didn't seem to help.

We made our way through the Palace to a back entrance. Merytre assured me this was a shorter route than the way we had gone the day Sutem showed us the pleasure lake. It didn't feel much shorter to me, but at least it was cooler than walking all the way around the outside of the Palace. As we exited the building, my heart pounded even harder.

"Are you well?" Ettu asked. "You sound like you are breathing oddly."

Indeed I couldn't quite get a full breath. In the shade of a tree, I stopped and set my hand to my chest.

"Just give me a moment," I said.

They waited silently. It was much more peaceful out here. Nobody talking or laughing. No doors slamming. Just the shady tree and the sun shining high in a cloudless blue sky. The mud brick path beneath my sandals. The aroma from a nearby flower bed, faint but still enough to make my nose tingle. My heartbeat steadied and I finally felt like I could breathe. We walked on.

As the lake came into view, my nerves increased again. I tried to think of nothing but the slap of my sandals on the path. A wooden jetty led out over deeper water and a boat waited there for us, its flat deck reminding me of those we had sailed down the Great River.

Pharaoh wasn't here yet. I was hardly surprised. I knew enough about him by now to understand he would likely keep me waiting so he could make a grand arrival.

We reached the lake and Ettu fussed over my appearance, straightening my gown and smoothing back a few stray hairs. She studied my makeup with a critical eye, but seemed satisfied with it. Then there was nothing else to do but wait under a shady tree.

"We should have brought you a chair," Ettu said.

"I can sit on the grass if I need to."

"You might stain your gown." She glanced back towards the Palace as if estimating how long it might take her to get there and back. "Perhaps I should go ask for a chair to be brought down."

"I'm sure he won't be much longer," I said, although we all knew it was probably a lie.

"My lady." Merytre's voice was hesitant. "Another Ornament approaches."

Indeed, someone else was making their way to the lake, trailed by two maids. I recognised Ishtar's profile immediately and a flicker of annoyance burned within me.

"Marduk, save me," I muttered. Was I not even to have this much time alone with Pharaoh? Would he again ignore me in favour of my sister?

"Surely not," Ettu said. "Has she no shame?"

"I suppose he invited her." Why did I feel the need to defend her? I was angry with her, wasn't I? But she was still my sister and she had been treated terribly. Resentment warred with sympathy, and I wasn't sure which was the stronger.

"There is someone else too." Merytre shaded her eyes as she peered towards where another woman had just left the Palace. "Lady Kia, I think."

The Ornament who followed Ishtar was not one whose face I recognised. I remember someone mentioning Kia before, though. Some gossip about a woman who claimed Pharaoh had given her an expensive gift but she refused to show it to anyone. I couldn't quite remember whether Kia was the one who received the gift or the one who wanted to see it.

I could tell the moment Ishtar recognised me, for her whole posture stiffened and she hesitated, as if wondering whether to turn back. But she kept walking and soon enough she stood in front of me. Belet-ili and another maid I didn't recognise were at her heels. Belet-ili studiously avoided meeting my eyes.

This close, the earthy scent of frankincense that wafted off Ishtar wrapped itself around me. It had been applied so liberally I wouldn't have been surprised if the cloud of scent rising from her was visible. My nose tingled and I sneezed.

Ishtar wore an elegant purple gown I'd never seen before. Maybe it had been specially made for her now she was an Ornament. I searched for something to say that wouldn't reveal how displeased I was at her arrival.

"Sister," Ishtar said. "Are you not even going to greet me?"

"Equally, you could greet me," I said, my voice cool. I was being unfair, though. This was Pharaoh's fault, not Ishtar's. He was the one who apparently couldn't stand to have the company of only one woman at at time.

"I suppose you are here to sail with Pharaoh," she said. "He invited me too."

"And her." I nodded towards the woman who was making her way along the last stretch of path, followed by several maids. Ishtar frowned as she turned to see who it was.

The woman looked to be a mix of Egyptian and something else that gave her a paler skin than most of the women here, Greek maybe. She was petite and delicate looking, with a face that was truly lovely and braids that hung to her waist.

Like Ishtar, Kia arrived in a cloud of perfume. The pungent aroma of jasmine was unmistakable. My head throbbed from the competing scents and I sneezed again. As Kia reached us, she gave both Ishtar and I a haughty glare.

"I suppose none of us knew Pharaoh was inviting anyone else," I said, trying to sound unbothered.

I was about to introduce myself, but Kia sniffed and looked away, and I changed my mind. Ishtar said nothing, although I knew her well enough to recognise the expression on her face as meaning she was scheming. She was figuring out how she could make the best of the situation.

"Here he comes," Ettu said softly.

Indeed, Pharaoh had appeared around the corner of the Palace. He wore a linen shirt and a *shendyt*, and a wig with shoulder-length braids. His arms were wreathed in what must be too many silver and gold bangles to feel comfortable. The metal would be hot against his skin on a day like this. A squad of guards surrounded him and an assortment of servants trailed behind. At least he didn't seem to have brought any almost-naked women with him today.

I fixed a smile on my face. This was my first real opportunity to get his attention. I would be pleasant and cheerful, enthusiastic and accommodating. All the things he would expect. As he drew closer, both Ishtar and Kia lay down on their bellies on the grass. I followed their example, although a heartbeat too slow. He had probably already noticed I didn't expect to prostrate myself.

"Well," Pharaoh said as he reached us. A long pause followed and I itched to know what he was doing. Was he merely standing there for the sake of leaving us lying on our bellies? At last, he grunted.

"You may rise," he said.

I quickly got to my feet and smoothed the front of my skirt. A few blades of grass clung to it and I wondered whether I had grass on my face or in my hair. I could almost feel Ettu restraining herself from rushing forward to tidy me.

The servants were preparing the boat, which seemed to mean arranging numerous cushions over the deck and erecting a shade sail. A large covered basket probably held food and drink. My stomach growled at the thought, reminding me I had been too nervous to eat much this morning.

Pharaoh said nothing further to us, only made his way out along the jetty. Were we supposed to follow him or wait for an invitation? Ishtar and I exchanged glances, and I was relieved she seemed as uncertain as me. At least I wasn't the only one who wasn't sure how to act around him. Kia seemed to have no such compunctions, only straightened her skirt one last time, then started after Pharaoh. Her maids found themselves shady places on the grass to sit and wait.

I nodded towards Ettu and Merytre, indicating they should do as the other maids did, then followed Kia. If she wasn't waiting for an invitation, I wouldn't either.

CHAPTER 32

Ishtar hurried to walk beside me as we made our way to the boat. I quickened my pace, not wanting to arrive with her and give Pharaoh another opportunity to choose between us, but she kept up with me. We reached the end of the jetty together. Kia was already there, flicking her braids around. Pharaoh was busy settling himself on a pile of cushions and seemed to take no notice of any of us.

A man, who I presumed by the way he held himself was a guard, offered his hand to Kia and helped her into the boat. Ishtar and I rushed forward, and I guessed she, like me, didn't want to be the last to board. We reached the guard together and he glanced at both of us before offering his hand to Ishtar. I took a deep breath and waited my turn. Of course he would choose Ishtar over me.

The guard steadied me as I stepped over the gap at the end of the jetty. The boat shifted just as I set my foot down and I stumbled a little. My cheeks heated, but nobody seemed to be paying any attention to me and even the guard had already looked away, his gaze drawn by Ishtar who had positioned herself on a cushion right next to Pharaoh and seemed to be whispering into his ear.

I was mollified to see Pharaoh didn't seem to be taking any notice of whatever Ishtar whispered to him. A servant woman was already pouring wine and another offered him a tray of delicacies, which he took his time selecting from. Ishtar frowned a little, said something else, and he finally turned his attention to her briefly. It was no more than a look and a slight inclination which might have been a nod, but it was enough for Ishtar. She leaned back on her cushion, an expression of satisfaction on her face.

Kia had claimed the spot on the other side of Pharaoh and I had to content myself with the cushion at his feet. A guard untied the rope securing the boat to the dock and others began to row us out to the centre of the lake. A servant offered me wine and I accepted a goblet, although I wasn't thirsty. At least it would give me something to do while Ishtar and Kia competed for Pharaoh's attention.

A light breeze whisked the sweat from my neck. Kia complimented Pharaoh on some decision or pronouncement or something. If she mentioned any detail, I missed it, but it seemed both she and Ishtar knew all about it.

"Yes, yes," he said. "We have to be careful with such people. They could be dangerous to us."

"Very dangerous," Kia said.

"I don't believe anyone else would have managed the situation quite like that," he said. "My advisors said I should send them to the slave mines, but personally I couldn't see the point. Why not make use of so many extra slaves here? And some of the women are quite beautiful. Primitive, of course, but beautiful in their own way."

"You are wise indeed." Ishtar leaned towards him and fluttered her eyelashes in a way that would have looked ridiculous on anyone else.

"It amazes me every day how wise you are." Kia placed her hand on his leg, seeking to draw his rapt attention away from Ishtar.

I watched the ripples the boat made as it moved through the water and tried not to roll my eyes. Could they hear themselves? Did they realise how ludicrous they sounded? And he was no better than they. Worse, in fact, because he encouraged them.

Did Father know what kind of man Pharaoh was? Surely he wouldn't have sent a daughter to marry him if he had known anything of the man's character. It reflected poorly on Father. If he didn't know what sort of man Pharaoh was, he should have found out before he sent either of us here.

We reached the lake's centre and the guards set their oars aside, then slipped into the water. They swam away, leaving the boat to drift with just Pharaoh, we three Ornaments, and the two serving women onboard. I kept my gaze on the water and tried not to listen to Ishtar and Kia's flattery.

A family of silver fish — perch, I thought — swam beside us for a while, then darted off in another direction. A pair of ducks cavorted nearby. Insects buzzed. The sun was warm on my skin. If it wasn't for the constant drone of Ishtar and Kia praising Pharaoh, it would have been quite peaceful out here.

"And what of you?" Pharaoh's voice suddenly broke through my daze. I looked up to find all three of them staring at me.

"Me?" Had he actually noticed me sitting silently at his feet?

"You have not yet said it was a fine decision," Pharaoh said.

"I'm afraid I am not familiar with the details."

"Oh, you don't need to understand it." He waved his hand dismissively in my direction. "You only need to know it was a good decision."

"But what did you actually decide?"

"It was about the prisoners. The ones captured in Kush."

He stopped to gulp his wine. Did he mean the folk like Abar and her sister, Atahar? Maybe he could tell me where Atahar was.

"What is to happen to them?" I asked.

"They will stay here in Thebes as slaves. They will remain in the positions they have been assigned to."

He gave me an incredulous look, before rolling his eyes at Ishtar. She giggled obediently and my traitorous cheeks flushed.

"But don't feel bad if you don't understand." He graced me with a condescending look. "Nobody expects a woman to understand such a thing."

"How would someone find out where a prisoner has been assigned?" I asked.

Another dismissive wave in my direction. "I have people who look after things like that."

"So if I wanted to find out where a particular prisoner is, who would I talk to?"

"I don't concern myself with that sort of detail."

He cared so little for the welfare of women stolen from their home country that he didn't even know how they were kept track of. Gone were any last illusions that Pharaoh might yet reveal himself to be wise and knowledgeable. He was a nasty, boastful fellow. Exactly the kind of man I would never choose for myself

"Did you receive the gifts from my father?" I asked.

Maybe if I could change the subject and discuss something

other than his newly captured slaves, I could get through the afternoon without revealing how much I despised him.

"You would have to ask my administrator," Pharaoh said.

"My father sent five ships filled with valuable goods. Surely you know whether you received them?"

He made a show of sighing and took another mouthful of wine before he replied.

"Who is your father then?" he asked.

"Marduk-apla-iddina of Babylon." I didn't bother to try to conceal the frostiness in my tone. He was too self absorbed to notice anyway. "You signed an alliance with him. My father sent me to marry you as part of the treaty."

"Oh, yes, the alliance with Babylon."

I waited while he had more wine.

"Yes, we have an agreement," he said. "No war against the other signatory, and so on."

"So you received the gifts he sent you?"

"Certainly. My advisors would have taken possession of them. They would have been recorded and stored appropriately."

I gave up and turned back to the water so I could roll my eyes without him seeing. What was the point of Father sending so many treasures if Pharaoh never even bothered to so much as review a list of what was sent? Now that I had given up asking such apparently unreasonable questions, Ishtar and Kia were quick to resume their attempts to focus his attention on themselves.

I tuned out their banal chatter and studied the insects that flittered across the lake's surface. I sipped my wine sparingly. If nothing else, it gave me one more thing to focus my attention on while I tried not to show anyone how much I loathed Pharaoh.

I had promised Tall and Half I would demand they be returned to me as soon as I met with Pharaoh, and I tried to find the right words to ask. It was only when someone squeaked, that I turned back to them.

Pharaoh held Kia by her wrist, squeezing it with such force that her whole hand had turned white. Her eyes bulged and she whimpered.

"Please," she whispered. "Forgive me."

"You're hurting her," I said.

If Pharaoh even heard me, he didn't respond. His attention was focussed on his fingers around Kia's wrist. An almost disinterested look on his face concealed whatever he was thinking as he squeezed her. Tears ran freely down her face.

"I heard the funniest thing yesterday," Ishtar said. It was an obvious attempt to distract him, but he didn't seem to notice.

A gust of wind caught the sail and the boat rocked. My wine spilled, landing on the deck with a splash. Pharaoh finally released his hold on Kia to snatch at his wig before it could be blown from his head. She cradled her hand to her chest, tears still running down her cheeks. Ishtar used her hem to dab at the wine in her lap, but the red stain only spread further. She huffed in exasperation.

Another gust of wind hit the boat and it rocked even more sharply. Ishtar squealed and dropped her goblet as she reached for something to hold onto. I tried to steady myself, my goblet already rolling across the deck. A stream of wine followed it, spreading over the timber like spilled blood.

The wind blew again, even stronger. Pharaoh bellowed for the servants to do something, but the women clutched each other and the boat, and seemed frozen in terror. Jugs of wine and plates of food slid across the deck.

It seemed almost inevitable when the wind blew again and

the boat tipped higher and higher. It happened so slowly I could almost see what would occur before it did. I was thrown from the deck and landed in the water, its warmth shocking after the relative coolness of the breeze. As I sank, my skirts tangled around my legs.

Trying to restrain my panic, I fought to free myself. I was almost out of air as I finally untangled my legs and kicked back up to the surface. I gasped for air as I took in the chaotic scene.

The boat had righted itself, a sole servant woman clinging to the mask. Slices of bread drifted on the water. As I searched for Ishtar, she surfaced and began swimming towards the shore.

Pharaoh was the next to appear, his face red and his wig gone. His arms thrashed ineffectively as he dipped beneath the surface again.

"Help me," he cried as he came back up. "I can't swim."

CHAPTER 33

J swam towards Pharaoh and he reached for me as
he saw me approaching. He was too panicked. If he
grabbed me, he would sink us both. I got behind him,
thinking it would let me stay out of his grasp, but didn't know
how to hold him. His waist was far too big and if I took his
arm, he would only grab me with the other, and we would
both go under. Not knowing what else to do, I hooked my
arm around his neck.

He grabbed me, digging his fingernails into my skin. His
considerable weight, although buoyed by the water, might
have been manageable for me, but he wriggled and thrashed
as if I was trying to murder him. I was so occupied in trying
to keep hold of him without letting him drag us both under,
that I couldn't move him.

"My lord," I said. "You must hold still. I can't get you to
shore like this."

"I can't swim," he cried.

I gritted my teeth and hung onto him. Kicking as hard as I
could, I managed to move him a little. Then guards were

there, taking him from me. It took three of them to subdue him enough to tow him to shore. The fourth stayed with me.

"Go," I said. "I can swim. There are others who need help."

He swam away and I searched the lake for Kia. Maybe she had already returned to shore? I could see Ishtar on the bank, but not her. Perhaps she couldn't swim. I took a deep breath and ducked beneath the surface. No sign of Kia, but the water was murky. She could be not very far away from me and I still mightn't see her.

I searched until I couldn't hold my breath anymore. I returned to the surface to take a few breaths, then ducked under again.

A flash of white beneath me. Was that her? I swam down, but had to return to the surface before I could be sure. I came back up not far from a guard.

"Somebody at the bottom of the lake," I called to him. "Right beneath me."

He signalled to another guard and they both dived.

I waited, gasping for breath. My legs were already tired, but I had to know if it was Kia down there.

Water splashed me in the face as the guards burst back up. They held Kia between them, limp and lifeless. One started swimming to shore with her. Her long braids trailed behind her in the water. I wondered absently how her wig could still be in place.

Then fear tore through me, sudden and alarming. With all that had been happening, I hadn't been scared before. There had been too much to do. But a woman was dead — an Ornament — and I couldn't catch my breath and my legs were so tired, I could hardly move them.

A guard appeared in front of me.

"Come," he said. "I'll help you to shore."

"No, I— I can do it. There are others who need help."

"Everyone else is being looked after. Let me help you."

My feet suddenly stopped moving and for a moment I couldn't remember how to swim. He was quick to grab me and turn me around so he could tow me behind him, his arm looped securely around my chest. I clung to his arm and looked up at the sky. It was just as blue as it had been when we set sail. When Kia was still alive. How easily that could have been me. Or Ishtar.

"There you go," the guard said. "You should be able to stand up now."

My legs wobbled as I found my footing. The lake's bottom was slimy with mud which seemed to wrap around my sandals, trying to hold me there in its waters. Ishtar was waiting for me as I staggered up the bank. Even with her soaked gown clinging to her body, her wig askew, and kohl running down her cheeks, she was beautiful.

"Sister," she cried and wrapped her arms around me. Her skin was cold but her body still held some warmth and I leaned into her gratefully. "Kia is dead and one of the serving women is missing."

My teeth chattered and I couldn't make any reply. Servants came to wrap blankets around our shoulders. I clutched Ishtar's arm, needing to feel the warmth of her skin and the beat of her pulse. She was alive. We both were. Thank Marduk we had learned to swim as children. I might never swim in the Purattu again, but it had saved my life today.

Kia's body was laid out on the grass, a blanket covering her. I tried not to look. Tried not to remember the flash of white at the bottom of the lake. I had never seen a dead body before. Less than an hour ago, Kia had been sitting on the boat, smiling and chatting to Pharaoh, trying to keep his attention. And now she was still and lifeless. I kept picturing her dead face, eyes open, mouth ajar, even though I never saw it.

Ishtar wept quietly, her hands over her face. I should probably hug her. Try to comfort her. But all I could do was stand there, holding her arm with one hand, my other clutching the blanket around my shoulders. Then I heard a familiar voice and somebody took me by the elbow.

"Come," he said. "I will take you back to your chambers."

"Khaemmalu." The gentleness in his voice made me cry. He squeezed my elbow and steered me across the grass. "I thought you weren't allowed to touch me."

It was a daft thing to say, but it came out of my mouth before I realised.

"I think Pharaoh will make an exception at a time like this," he said. "The administrators have called all guards on duty."

"My lady!"

Ettu's voice came from somewhere behind us. I had forgotten she and Merytre were waiting for me. Ettu embraced me firmly and Merytre squeezed my hand.

"I am sorry we couldn't come to you straight away," Ettu said. "Lady Kia's maids are hysterical and we were trying to calm them."

"We saw what you did." Merytre's voice was admiring. "We were watching as the boat tipped over and we saw you save Pharaoh."

"Marduk, my heart beat so hard I thought it would burst right out of my chest," Ettu said. "I have never been so relieved as when I saw your head come up out of the water."

"I barely remember what happened now," I said. "It's all confused."

A gust of wind caught my blanket, threatening to tear it from me. My teeth chattered.

"We need to get you out of those wet things," Ettu said, then to Khaemmalu, "We can take her from here."

"I feel rather odd," I said just before my knees buckled.

Khaemmalu grabbed me before I hit the ground and swept me up in his arms.

"Show me the way," he said to my maids.

His arms around me were strong and his chest was so warm. I needed warmth. Hardly knowing what I did, I rested my head on his shoulder and closed my eyes. All I knew of the journey back to my chambers was darkness and warmth and the knowledge that I was safe in Khaemmalu's arms.

I was jarred from my peaceful cocoon when he lay me on a couch. I opened my eyes, but the chamber was too bright and I closed them again. Merytre was telling Ahmose what had happened, and Ettu and Khaemmalu talked quietly, their voices no more than a murmur in the background. Then the sound of the door closing and Ettu urging me to sit up. When I opened my eyes, Khaemmalu was gone.

"Come on," Ettu said. "We need to get you out of that sodden gown. Merytre has more blankets, and Ahmose is making you some tea. Just sit up and let me get this gown off."

Between her and Merytre, they somehow undressed me, although I must have been of no help to them. They wrapped blankets around me and sat me back on the couch. By then, Ahmose had her tea ready and she pressed a warm mug into my hands.

"Drink it all," she said. "It has herbs to warm you and calm your nerves."

"Did you hear about Kia?" I asked, or at least I meant to. What came out of my mouth was no more than a groan.

"Don't fuss," Ahmose said. "You are safe here and you will feel much better once you drink this."

She wrapped my fingers around the mug and helped me raise it to my mouth. I managed to sip a little. The warm liquid slipped down my throat, leaving a trail of warmth behind it. I could feel it all the way down to my belly.

"What is wrong with her?" Merytre asked. "Did she get too much water in her lungs?"

"She wasn't under for that long," Ettu said. "And she and Lady Ishtar were the only ones who knew how to swim apart from the guards."

"It is the shock," Ahmose said. "It is making her feel cold and confused. We need to warm her, and keep her quiet and still. She will recover soon enough."

She kept urging me to drink and eventually the mug was empty. They helped me lie down, with a cushion under my head and another blanket draped over the ones wrapped around me. The hot tea had thawed my cold insides and its warmth spread through my whole body. Darkness seemed to creep up over me and then I knew nothing else.

CHAPTER 34

The chamber was dark when I woke, lit only by a lamp turned down low. I must have made some noise because Ettu was quickly at my side.

"My lady, how do you feel?" she asked.

I struggled to sit up, swaddled tightly as I was in blankets. She helped me up and for a moment I just sat there. My head spun a little, but quickly settled.

"Much better," I said. "I am warm now and my teeth have stopped chattering."

"Ahmose said you were in shock. She has gone to bed, but she said you should drink more tea when you woke. Here."

She poured from a jug which was wrapped in towels to keep its contents from cooling and handed me the mug. My head cleared some more as I sipped the warm tea.

"Is there any news?" I asked. "The last I heard, one of the serving women was missing."

"She has not been found yet, as far as I know. Pharaoh has returned to his palace. Lady Kia's maids were both over-wrought and a healer had to be called. That is all we have heard so far. Merytre and Ahmose went out earlier to ask around."

The memory of warm arms around me returned. I hesitated to ask, but I had to know whether I had dreamed it.

"Did Khaemmalu really carry me back?" I asked.

"Yes, he and Sutem were given special dispensations to see you and Lady Ishtar to your chambers. It was a good thing too, since neither of you were fit to walk."

"Is Ishtar well?"

"We haven't heard any word of her, but she seemed well enough the last I saw her. Sutem would have made sure she got there safely."

"Would you send someone to check?"

"Of course."

I was surprised to find my mug already empty. I had drunk all the tea without realising. It had made me feel much better.

"And Kia?" I asked. "What will happen to her?"

"She will be looked after by the priests in the House of Life. Apparently there is a very lengthy process to prepare a body for burial. Ahmose can tell you about it, if you want. She told me a little and it is rather gruesome."

"Is someone sending word to her family?"

"The administrators will take care of that."

"Does she have no friends here? Is there nobody who could draft a message that would be more personal than what Panouk would send?"

"There isn't anyone she is particularly friendly with, as far as I know," Ettu said. "She seems to have kept to herself."

"What a shame."

Fatigue washed over me and I could hardly keep my eyes open.

"You should get some more sleep," Ettu said. "Let me help you to your bedchamber."

I was cozy on the couch, wrapped in blankets.

"No, I'll just stay here," I said.

She positioned a stool beneath my feet and I rested my head against the back of the couch. When I next woke, it was well after dawn. Merytre stood looking out a window and Ahmose was perched on a nearby chair, her broken arm propped up on a cushion.

"Your face is a much better colour," Ahmose said when she noticed I was awake. "You were as white as milk yesterday."

"I feel better. The tea helped."

I struggled to stand up with the blankets wrapped tightly around my legs. I knocked over the stool that had been under my feet and almost toppled over myself before Merytre came to help me. As she unwound the blankets, I realised I was naked beneath them.

"We had enough trouble getting you undressed," Merytre said, noticing my surprise. "It didn't seem necessary to dress you again when we were going to wrap the blankets around you anyway."

I waved away her explanation and staggered down the hallway to my bedchamber, clutching the last blanket around my shoulders. Someone had laid out my sleeping gown on the bed. I dropped the blanket and pulled the gown over my head. It was only then I realised I wasn't wearing a wig. I remembered noticing Ishtar's being all out of place, but had no memory of what happened to my own.

"Did I lose my wig in the water?" I asked when I returned to the sitting chamber.

"You weren't wearing it when you came to shore," Merytre said. "I can go ask if anyone found it."

"No, don't worry about it."

There were more important things to be done than finding my wig. It wasn't like I didn't have at least a dozen others anyway.

"Ettu sent word last night to your lady's maids that you wouldn't need them this morning," she said. "Ahmose said you should have a quiet day with as little excitement as possible."

"That would be most welcome." Any excuse to avoid being stripped naked in front of so many women was welcome.

Servants brought breakfast and Merytre insisted I sit on the couch and tell her what I wanted. My stomach grumbled and I realised I missed dinner last night. Ettu emerged from her bedchamber, yawning. She and Merytre must have taken turns to sit with me through the night. As I ate, I asked Ahmose how her arm was.

"The pain has lessened," she said. "Although it still hurts if I move it much. As long as I keep it still, I hardly notice it anymore."

"How long will it take to heal?" I asked around a mouthful of bread.

"A few weeks. I check it every couple of days when I replace the bandages. The swelling has gone down and the bruising is fading."

"I'm pleased it doesn't hurt too much anymore," I said. "Who would like to join me for a walk after breakfast?"

"Oh, no," Ettu said quickly. "Ahmose said you need to rest."

"I feel perfectly well."

I wasn't going to tell them I hoped Khaemmalu might be out there somewhere. But all three women insisted I was to stay in my chamber today and I had to console myself with the thought that he was probably on night shift anyway. I wondered how he got here so quickly yesterday if he was off duty. Maybe he happened to be in the grounds for some reason, or maybe he lived nearby. I didn't even know where he lived.

I sent Ettu and Merytre out to ask if there was any more news and they returned with the sad tidings that the body of the missing servant woman had been retrieved from the lake.

"Folk are saying there was magic used." Ettu's voice made it clear what she thought of the possibility.

"It was the wind," I said. "Anyone who was there could see that."

"But it was an unusually strong wind," Merytre said. "Folk say such a wind has never been seen here before, and certainly not on the pleasure lake, sheltered as it is by the trees and the wall."

Now she put it that way, it did seem a little odd the wind could have been so strong.

"But magic?" I asked. "Is that really possible?"

We all looked to Ahmose, since she was the only one of us with arcane knowledge. She gave us a shrug.

"If one knew the correct spell, I don't see why not," she said.

"Do you know any spells that could do such a thing?" I asked.

"Not I," she said. "But a person could create such a spell even if they didn't already know one. It might take some trial and error, though."

"But to what purpose?" Ettu asked. "It makes no sense."

"Maybe whoever made the spell didn't mean for the wind to be so strong," Merytre suggested. "They might have just wanted to cause a bit of confusion, knock the boat around."

"Or they wanted to kill someone and the strong wind was intentional," Ahmose said.

"You think someone *wanted* to tip the boat?" Ettu asked. "With Pharaoh onboard?"

Now I had spent some time with him, I could see why he might be targeted in such a way. Apart from being pompous, he was also cruel. I hadn't yet forgotten Kia's squeak of pain as he squeezed her wrist, or the way Ishtar flinched away from me when I tried to examine her bruised neck.

"Pharaoh wasn't the only person on that boat," Ahmose said. "And he might not have been the intended victim."

"Are you saying someone could have been targeting Ishtar or me?" I asked. "Or Kia?"

It seemed an impossible idea. Surely none of us had done anything to provoke an enemy so determined to kill us. Ahmose only shrugged again.

"I have no idea. I am merely presenting another possibility. If Lady Kia was the target, then the spell was a success. But unless we can find out who is responsible, we have no way of identifying who the victim was supposed to be."

"It can't have been Lady Kassaya," Ettu said. "She has been nothing but kind to the women she has met here. And Lady Ishtar..."

Her voice trailed away.

"Ishtar hasn't been unkind to anyone," I said.

"No, but she also hasn't won herself any friends with the way she so immediately attracted Pharaoh's attention," Ettu said.

"But there was nothing malicious about that," I said. "It was just Ishtar being Ishtar."

"I know that. But plenty of women here would feel threatened by such a thing, and from a newcomer."

"Like Tiye?" I asked.

Ettu shrugged.

"No," I said. "Surely not."

"I know you have become friendly with her, but I don't think you should trust her," she said. "Never forget what she told you she did to the woman who was Top Ornament when she arrived."

"Ishtar isn't anywhere near taking Tiye's place as Top Ornament," I said.

"Lady Tiye isn't the only possibility," Merytre said. "Almost any Ornament could feel aggrieved enough at a newcomer to want to remove her. I agree Lady Tiye isn't to be trusted, but I think the same could be said for any of them. And nobody would have known you and Lady Ishtar could swim."

"We don't even know it was really a spell," I said. "It's just as likely to have been a freak wind that blew on exactly the right angle to come in over the walls and tip the boat."

"It is possible," Ahmose said. "Even if unlikely. I agree a spell seems the most probable cause, and I don't think we can rule out either Pharaoh or any of the Ornaments who were onboard as the intended victim."

"How would we find out?" I asked. "Would such a spell leave any trace?"

Ahmose shook her head.

"There is no way to know," she said. "Not unless the spell's creator confesses."

CHAPTER 35

Around the middle of the day, I was standing at a window, hoping to see Khaemmalu, when someone rapped smartly on the door. Ettu opened the door to find a messenger boy there.

"Message from Pharaoh, Mighty Bull, Strong and Valiant like Montu, Rich in Years Like Ptah, the King of Upper and Lower Egypt," he announced, his chest puffed out with self importance.

"Go on," said Ettu, sounding unimpressed.

"Pharaoh invites Lady Kassaya from Babylon to a banquet at his palace in four days," the boy said.

"My lady would be pleased to accept," Ettu said.

She closed the door and raised her eyebrows at me.

"Well," she said. "It seems all you had to do to get Pharaoh's attention was save his life."

"I hardly saved his life," I said, shaking my head as I turned back to the window. Still no sign of Khaemmalu. I knew there wouldn't be. Not at this time of day.

"You kept his head above water until the guards got to him," Merytre said.

"There were so many guards," I said. "Someone would have gotten to him very shortly, probably even sooner if I wasn't there."

"No, they went straight to him," Ettu said. "Pharaoh was their first priority, as you would expect. They only went to help others once they had him safe. But if you hadn't been there, he might have drowned. They did have to swim quite a long way."

"I looked for Kia," I said, "but it was too late."

"There was nothing anyone could have done," she said. "One of the guards who retrieved her said her skirt was all tangled around her legs. She had kicked a hole in it and her sandal was caught. Even if she knew how to swim, she wouldn't have been able to do anything, tangled like that."

Her words reminded me of how my skirt had wrapped around my legs. I, too, sank under the water and fought to free myself. It could have been me who was found on the bottom of the lake. If I hadn't, by some accident, managed to untangle my skirt. If I didn't know how to swim. It would have been so easy.

"But you saved Pharaoh." Ettu sounded like she forced a cheerfulness she didn't feel into her voice. "And it seems he intends to thank you for it."

I scoffed. Even if he had noticed my actions, I doubted he would thank me. More likely, he would find a way to take credit for it himself. After all, who else but Pharaoh could have done such a marvellous thing?

"This is your chance," Ettu said. "You've got his attention now and you need to make the most of it."

"What will she wear?" Merytre asked.

"We will send for the sewers," Ettu said. "Four days is plenty of time to make something new."

Within the hour, my chamber filled with a team of sewers who took my measurements and argued with Ettu and Merytre about what they would make. It seemed everyone had a firm idea of what I should wear, and no two women agreed. Their bickering made my head hurt, so I went back to the window. I breathed in the fresh air and tried not to hear the argument behind me. Eventually, I couldn't take it anymore.

"Ettu will make the decision," I said, turning to give them all a glare. "She is in charge of my maids and she will decide what I am to wear."

The sewers muttered apologies and soon departed with a promise to have a design ready for Ettu's approval by morning. As the door closed behind them, I breathed a sigh of relief. Finally, the chamber was peaceful again.

"It would have been much easier for me to wear something I already have," I said. "There are chests of gowns in there, most of which I have never even seen."

"But the gowns you brought with you are Babylonian fashions," Ettu said. "They were made for Ishtar anyway. The women here dress differently and you have worn all your Egyptian gowns at least once. We can't send you off to a banquet with Pharaoh wearing an old gown."

"I hardly think the fact that I have worn a gown once makes it old," I said. "And he has only seen two of them anyway."

I doubted he even noticed what I had worn the times I had met him, but kept that to myself.

"I agree with Ettu," Merytre said. "You need a new gown. Something very fine."

"There was a time when you wouldn't have ventured an opinion," I said to her.

"I'm sorry, my lady," Merytre said quickly. "Of course it isn't my place to give my opinion."

"No, I'm the one who is sorry," I said. "I didn't mean you shouldn't. We all speak our minds here, especially Ettu."

I gave Ettu a pretend glare, hoping to lighten the mood, and Merytre smiled weakly, although she didn't seem convinced.

"I am going to look through your jewels," Ettu said. "And set aside some possibilities for you to wear. We won't be able to make any decisions until we see the final design for your gown, but I want to be prepared."

"I'll help you," Merytre said, and the two of them went off together.

I sank down onto the couch and met Ahmose's gaze. The old woman was in her usual spot with her arm propped up. It was the first opportunity I'd had to speak with her in private since yesterday's incident.

"What do you really think?" I asked her. "About the possibility that a spell caused the wind?"

"Just as I said. It could be, or it might not be. We have no way of knowing."

"Do you know anyone here who might be casting spells?" I asked.

"I have been wracking my brain about that. One of the priestesses maybe. But equally, it could be an Ornament or a serving woman. There are women here from all over the world. Surely, I am not the only one with knowledge of arcane matters."

"You said you could teach me about such things," I said. "Before we left Babylon."

I still needed to convince her to show me how to make the potion that let us slip past the guards.

"I did." She looked at me evenly. "Are you sure you really want such knowledge, though? Folk make assumptions about those who know things that others don't. Even if you only know a little, they always think you know more than you do. When things happen, they will blame you."

"Do you think someone might accuse you of spelling the wind?"

Surely nobody would think one of my own servants was responsible, given that I, too, was on the boat. Ahmose shook her head.

"I have been careful to keep my knowledge to myself," she said. "Only those who share these chambers are aware of it."

"What about your suppliers? Whoever you are sourcing all your herbs and things from?"

"Most of what I use has medicinal purposes. Curing headaches and loose bowels, and the like. I have often mentioned that someone is vomiting or has a sore eye or whatever when I have sought out new herbs. There is only one item in my possession that can't be explained as having a medicinal purpose."

"So what of the person you got that from? Might they be suspicious?"

"Perhaps," she said with a shrug. "But I might be equally suspicious of them for having access to such a thing."

"What do you use it for, this thing that has no medical purpose?"

"It is a key ingredient in the potion that allows us to walk past the guards without being seen."

"Is it possible the person you source it from might guess that's what you're using it for?"

She frowned. "I wouldn't think so, not unless there were rumours about such a potion being used. If that happened, she might guess. If she knew enough about what such a herb can do with the right combination of ingredients."

"Khaemmalu knows you leave the grounds. You and Ettu both."

"I suppose we can only pray he keeps such knowledge to himself then," she said. "It could cause trouble for all of us if he were to tell anyone, especially now there is suspicion about the use of spells within the Palace."

"I don't think anyone should go out again," I said. "Not for a while at least. We should let everything settle first."

In the days leading up to Pharaoh's banquet, I kept to my usual schedule to avoid any unnecessary attention. I ate breakfast in the dining chamber most days with Henutmire, and sometimes Gilukhipa and Ineni, followed by a short visit to Tiye. In the afternoons, I strolled through the gardens, accompanied by either Ettu or Merytre, and tried to pretend to myself I wasn't watching for Khaemmalu.

The sewers presented their proposed design to Ettu and after discussing something she wanted changed, they went off to make my gown. They brought it for me to try on a day later, once the fabric was cut and pinned together, a thoroughly tiresome activity that resulted in me being jabbed many times before they managed to get it off me again.

On the morning of the banquet, my entire team of maids came to bathe and shave me. They rubbed perfumed ointment over every bit of my skin, making me sneeze so violently that they ended up bathing me again to remove the scent, and then applying less of the lotions. By the time they finished, my nose was running, but at least I wasn't still sneezing. They filed and painted my nails and even scrubbed some hard callouses from my heels, despite my protests that Pharaoh would hardly be looking at the bottom of my feet.

It was midafternoon by the time they began dressing me and making up my face. At long last, they pronounced me ready and crowded around to see my reaction when Ettu passed me the hand mirror. For all the hours they had spent primping me, I couldn't see much difference from how I usually looked, although I could hardly tell them that. Instead I pronounced myself very satisfied and they were full of smiles as they filed out the door.

"You do look lovely, my lady," Ettu said.

"I thought they would never finish," I grumbled. "I don't suppose I have time to eat something?"

"I'm afraid not. Your transport is due at dusk so you should start heading down to the gates. Besides, we would have to do your makeup again before you left and I suspect you'd rather not endure that."

"My lady." Ahmose pressed a small linen packet into my hand. "Put this in your pouch. Empty the contents into Pharaoh's wine, but only if you can be sure of doing it without anyone seeing. The last thing we need right now is any suspicion pointed at you."

"What is it?" I asked, tucking the little packet away.

"A love potion, of sorts," she said. "It will enhance Pharaoh's virility and make it more likely that if he beds you tonight, you will bear a babe."

"Do you think he will expect me to… do that?" My cheeks already heated at the thought. "I thought this was a banquet? With other people?"

"The messenger said a banquet, yes," she replied. "He didn't say who else would be attending. Even if there are others present, this might be your chance. If you stay until everyone else is gone, Pharaoh might take his opportunity with you."

"Marduk, I wasn't expecting that tonight."

"You do... know what to do?" she asked, delicately.

I blushed even harder and looked down at my perfectly manicured fingernails, too embarrassed to meet her eyes. She had asked once before and I had said I did. I could hardly say now I was uncertain.

"Perhaps you would like me to tell you?" she suggested. "Just to be sure there is no confusion."

"I think that would be a good idea." I tried to sound confident, but I couldn't look at Ahmose as she explained what would happen when Pharaoh bedded me. Ettu and Merytre busied themselves on the other side of the chamber, and I appreciated them at least pretending they weren't listening.

"Marduk," I whispered when Ahmose finished. It was worse than I had thought.

"I can give you something to help you feel more relaxed," she said. "Or something that will make the process more agreeable for you."

"Unless you can give me something to make me unconscious, I think I shall just have to suffer through it."

"It won't be so bad," she said. "You will see."

"You must have..." My voice trailed away and I gestured, wordlessly.

"Yes," she said. "Many times. First with my husband, and that was not so bad. But then also with the man I was given to afterwards. That was... unpleasant."

Ettu went to open the door.

"My lady, you really need to leave," she said. "Come, Merytre and I will walk you to the gates."

"Bar the door behind us," I said to Ahmose.

"Good luck," she said. "I pray to Isis you will be with child when you return."

Ettu and Merytre were unusually quiet as we made our way through the Palace and along the path that led to the front gates. As the gates came into view, tall shadows which loomed against the darkening sky, I paused.

"Any last words of advice?" I asked.

Before they could reply, a familiar voice spoke from a nearby bush.

"Lady Kassaya."

"Khaemmalu, is that you?"

I stared hard at the bush but could see little behind the shadows.

"Go to the place where we have spoken before," he said.

"I cannot," I said. "I am on my way to Pharaoh's palace."

"You must," he said. "It is most urgent."

The bush rustled again and I sensed he was gone. The three of us looked at each other.

"What do I do?" I asked. "My transport is probably waiting."

"You told him you were going to see Pharaoh," Ettu said. "And he said to meet him anyway. That says to me that whatever it is, the matter is of the highest importance. He would not suggest you keep Pharaoh waiting for anything less than…"

"Life and death," Merytre finished grimly. "I agree with Ettu. You have to find out what he wants."

"Come on then," I said. "Maybe if we walk quickly, we can deal with whatever this is and I won't be too late."

"Pharaoh will be even later anyway," Ettu said.

We hurried along the path and soon found ourselves in

the sheltered spot where Khaemmalu found me after he discovered Ettu had left the grounds. I expected to hear him whispering to us from his hidden place, but it was Tall who spoke.

"Princess!" he said.

"Tall? What are you doing here?"

"Half!"

"What happened? Is he all right?"

"Here!"

"Come back here," Khaemmalu said. "Leave one of your maids to keep watch."

"Go," Merytre said to Ettu. "I'll watch for anyone nearby."

Ettu and I hurried around behind the shrubs. There, sitting on the ground with his back against a dom palm tree, was Half. Blood stained the front of his tunic, and his eyes were closed. In the silence of the grove, I could hear the rasp of his breath. Ettu let out a soft cry and dropped to her knees beside him. She raised her hand, but seemed afraid to touch him, and she let it fall again.

"What happened?" I asked.

Half only groaned.

"Knife!" Tall flapped his hands. "Belly!"

"Who did this?" I asked. "Tell me."

"Man!"

"Which man?"

"Man!"

"What language does he use?" Khaemmalu asked. "I have asked him what happened and could make no sense of his reply."

"He only speaks Babylonian." I hadn't even realised I had slipped into that language in response to Tall. "He says it was a man, but I don't think he knows who."

My mind whirled and I was barely aware of what I said as I tried to figure out how we could help Half.

"Tall, is there anything else you can tell us?" I asked.

"Danger!" His voice was mournful now. "Flee! Palace!"

"We need to get them to my chambers," I said. "Ahmose will be able to help."

Khaemmalu cleared his throat. "I'm sure you are aware—"

"I know," I said, cutting him off. "Whatever it is, let's just agree I already know. My only concern right now is how we can help Half."

"My lady, you need to go," Merytre reminded me. "You have already accepted Pharaoh's invitation and you cannot be late."

"I can't go now," I said. "Not with Half like this."

"Go," Khaemmalu said. "We will look after him."

I met his eyes, but saw nothing that told me I couldn't trust him.

"I will do what I can," he said before I could speak. "Leave your maids with me. I'm going to need all the help I can get if we are to smuggle two men into your chambers."

I hated leaving them, but Merytre was right. It would only draw attention if I didn't attend the banquet. With one last look at Half, I hurried along the path. The shadows stretching across it merged as the last of the sunlight disappeared.

My heart pounded as I tried to watch all directions at once in case someone lurked nearby. I had never before been alone in the gardens at night. Was this what Nebtu did before she disappeared? Did she too, for some unknown reason, go wandering alone? Relief surged through me as the gates came into sight. They were slightly ajar.

"Hello?" I called as I approached.

A guard appeared between the gates.

"Lady Kassaya?" he asked.

His face was familiar, and I guessed he must have been on duty the night we arrived here, but if he had told me his name, I couldn't remember it.

"Yes, it's me. I'm supposed to go to Pharaoh's palace. I'm afraid I am running rather late."

"We've been expecting you," he said. "Your transport is waiting."

A palanquin stood ready for me with ten slaves to bear it. Half as many guards waited to escort me, along with a man I assumed must be the slave master.

A guard helped me into the palanquin and I clutched the sides as the slaves raised it to their shoulders at a cry from their master. We set off, jerky at first until they found their rhythm. I finally released my hold on the side of the palanquin and clutched my hands in my lap. How would I get through the evening, not knowing whether Half lived or died? Could I really trust Khaemmalu to help, or had he turned them in as soon as I left? And what in Marduk's name had happened?

Tall had clearly witnessed the attack, but he might not be able to tell us any more than he already had. For the first time, I cursed Tall's inability to express himself, although I immediately felt bad about it. It wasn't his fault his words didn't come out the way he wanted them to, and it surely frustrated him as much as anyone else. Tall knew what had happened. I just had to figure out how to help him tell me.

CHAPTER 37

*B*usy as I was with fretting about Half, the journey to Pharaoh's palace was over almost before I noticed. The slaves set down the palanquin at the front door and a guard helped me out. I straightened my gown, wishing I had Ettu with me. She would fuss over my hair being wind-blown, wipe any smudges from my kohl, and be a supportive presence behind me. I would feel more confident if she was here with me.

"Welcome, Lady Kassaya." A portly man appeared in the doorway and bowed low from his waist. "I am Maharbaal, personal butler to Pharaoh. Please follow me."

He turned and waddled across the entrance chamber without waiting for a reply. I had thought the Palace of the Ornaments was richly decorated, but this place was truly ostentatious. Columns and doors made of electrum, windows lined with gold. Depictions of a man I assumed was Pharaoh covered every wall, always either engaged in acts of war or watching his army as it carried out its slaughter. He loomed over bound captives, an axe in his hand. He cut open the belly of one man and the throat of another. He shot an arrow into the back of a fleeing woman while her child watched nearby. So much death and destruction. What kind of man would want to be surrounded by such images?

As seemed typical for the art of these people, Pharaoh was always depicted several times larger than anyone else and although the face looked somewhat like him, the figure certainly didn't. He was always shown as a lean, muscled man in his prime. I wouldn't recognise him if I had only his portraits to identify him.

Maharbaal led me to an enormous dining hall filled with little tables. Both lamps and candles lit the hall and the air was already uncomfortably warm. Dozens of serving women waited, standing with their backs to the walls. I must be becoming accustomed to the mostly-naked women Pharaoh liked to attend him because this time the sight wasn't shocking to me.

What was shocking, however, was the acrobats — both male and female — who performed in the centre of the chamber. If they wore anything at all, it wasn't visible as they tumbled and cavorted. I averted my gaze so as not to see their most intimate parts.

At one end of the hall were a harpist and a lyre player, their music providing a pleasant backdrop to the scene. At the other end, a raised platform bore several little tables and it was there Maharbaal led me.

"Right here, please," he said, gesturing to a table. "Pharaoh honours you greatly tonight with a position so close to him."

I thanked him and sat on the cushion, tucking my legs to the side. Smoothing my skirt, I wished again that Ettu was with me. The hall was already filling with folk who all seemed to know each other. A few claimed their tables, but most stood in small groups, chatting and laughing. A serving woman brought a goblet of wine and I was thankful to have something to do while I sat there alone. None of the guests approached me, although I saw a few staring curiously.

As was usual for Pharaoh, he kept us waiting for quite some time. I tried not to fret about Half, but it was difficult when I had nothing else to do. I finished my wine and a serving woman brought more. The back of my neck was damp with sweat and the noise from the guests grew louder, some already sounding intoxicated.

I sipped my wine as slowly as I could, but even so, I had almost finished again before a commotion at the far end of the hall indicated Pharaoh's arrival. It was only then I noticed the guards who had taken up positions around the hall. Unlike the revellers, they took no wine, standing still and alert.

Pharaoh pranced through the hall, his head held high. Folk called greetings and blessings to him, but he ignored them all. Behind him came a woman who was so beautiful, she could have been a goddess. She was older than I expected. Not as old as Ahmose, but certainly older than Tiye by at least a few years. And, to my surprise, she was clearly not Egyptian. From her darker skin and the shape of her eyes, I guessed she might have been Syrian. She wore a sheer golden gown that hid no more of her body than the serving women's girdles. Silver chains decorated her throat and waist, and thick silver bands wound around her upper arms. Half a dozen maids followed her.

Pharaoh ignored me as he hauled himself up to the dais and took his seat. A guard positioned himself behind Pharaoh, one hand resting on the dagger at his waist. Serving women rushed to offer an assortment of wine bottles for him to choose from.

The beautiful woman settled herself next to him and her maids fussed over her, smoothing her skirt and ensuring she was comfortable, before they retreated. She gave me a cool look.

"The Ornament, I assume," she said.

"Kassaya, my lady," I said. "From Babylon."

"Aah, yes." She looked at me for a long moment and I waited, unsure whether I should say something else. "I believe there is an alliance. You were part of it, I assume?"

"I was sent in fulfilment of the alliance," I said, unsure whether she was asking if I had been involved in negotiating it. Surely not. What woman would offer herself as part of the terms?

She raised a goblet to her lips and looked at me steadily over the top as she drank.

"You are the one who pulled him from the water." It was an observation, not a question.

"Not exactly," I said. "I only kept his head above water. The guards pulled him out."

"Hmm."

The coolness in her tone puzzled me. She seemed almost… aggrieved I had helped.

"Are you the queen?" I blurted it out, not knowing what else to say. The way she stared was making me nervous.

She arched her eyebrows, reminding me of Tiye.

"I am Isis-Tahemdjeret. Queen of Egypt, Great Royal Wife, Lady of the Two Lands, the God's Wife, and one day, when Pharaoh becomes a hawk and flies off to heaven, the God's Mother. You may call me Lady Isis or Queen Isis."

I sipped my wine, hoping to cover my unease. Her list of titles was impressive, even more so because she wasn't Egyptian born, although I couldn't have said why that surprised me. Pharaoh had shown a predilection for foreign women and had no care as to whether they came to him willing or not. Was Lady Isis too sent to fulfil an alliance, or did she come to Pharaoh's attention in some other way? Did she want to be here? Would she have chosen another life for herself if she could have? She was queen, at least.

"I suppose you are waiting to be thanked."

Pharaoh's voice tore me from my thoughts. From how little notice he had taken of me the last two times I met him, I would have been unsurprised if he didn't speak to me at all, or if he didn't even remember me.

"Not at all, my lord," I said. "I was happy to be of service."

"My guards said I would have drowned before they could get to me," he said. "So I suppose we should thank you."

It was said with such obvious reluctance that I wondered why he even bothered.

"I appreciate you inviting me tonight," I said.

"Yes, well." He drained his goblet and held it up to be refilled. "You may consider this your reward."

"Thank you, my lord." It was an effort to make myself sound appreciative. Was it really that difficult for him to say something nice to the woman who had supposedly saved his life?

The aroma of roasted meat caught my attention and my stomach growled fiercely, reminding me I had eaten nothing today. Serving women began bringing an assortment of platters, which they offered first to Pharaoh, then to Isis, then me. The guard who stood behind Pharaoh was offered nothing, even though he was close enough to see every bite we took. We dined on a lavish assortment of roasted duck, hen, pig and fish, accompanied by a wide variety of vegetables, salads, breads and cheeses.

"Where is the halfwit?" Pharaoh bellowed suddenly and I jumped in surprise, almost knocking over my wine. He slapped his hand against the table. "Find the little funny fellow."

The guard behind him gestured and a young man hurried away. An administrator perhaps, or maybe just a servant. Whoever he was, he mustn't know Half wasn't here. Did anyone know? Was Half even still alive? Had they managed to get him to Ahmose? I could barely breathe as I waited for someone to say Half was gone.

As a serving woman came to top up my wine again, I remembered Ahmose's potion. I was supposed to drop it in Pharaoh's goblet. But how could I do that from where I sat? Beneath the table, I slipped the packet out of my pouch and waited until Pharaoh had a full goblet. I stood.

"I need to go outside for a moment," I said to the guard behind Pharaoh. "Is there someone who could take me?"

As he glanced over to gesture to one of the servants, I pretended to trip and fell against Pharaoh's table, knocking his goblet on its side.

"Oh, I am so sorry," I said. "How clumsy of me. Let me get you more wine."

Pharaoh shot me a glare, but I had managed to ensure the goblet fell away from him so he didn't get wet. I couldn't imagine how he would have reacted to a lap full of wine. I rushed to the bench where the wine bottles stood and quickly procured a new goblet. A serving woman insisted on filling it for me and as I turned back to Pharaoh, I tipped the packet into the wine. Ahmose hadn't said I would need to stir it and I could only pray that the contents, whatever they were, sank quickly.

"I am so sorry, my lord," I said as I set the goblet on his

table, which had already been wiped clean. "I have always been terribly clumsy."

He didn't look at me as he raised the goblet and took a few mouthfuls. The pounding of my heart drowned out the noise of the diners as I waited for him to comment on the wine tasting odd or having something floating in it, but he only set the goblet down and pointedly looked away from me.

I took my place again, trying not to look at Lady Isis, whose cool gaze still studied me. Had she seen me do it? If she had, it was already too late. I could only pray to Marduk she hadn't. If anyone remembered I had asked to go outside, they didn't mention it.

The man who had gone in search of Half returned and came to whisper to Pharaoh's guard. He nodded and the man hurried away.

"My lord," the guard said. "I'm afraid the funny man couldn't be found."

"What do you mean he can't be found?" Pharaoh shot him a glare over his shoulder. "Send someone else to find him."

The guard gestured again to the man who had searched for Half and a quick conversation passed between them, before the man disappeared again. Did this mean others would now be looking for him? Eventually they would have to realise he wasn't on the grounds. What would happen then? Did they know he was from Babylon? Would someone draw a connection between Half and me, and wonder whether I knew something about his unexpected disappearance?

The diners grew increasingly rowdy as the evening passed. The man who had gone in search of Half didn't return and Pharaoh didn't ask for him again. I felt uncomfortably full and waved away the servants who continued presenting platters to me. Pharaoh kept filling his plate, but Isis ate sparingly. I wondered how she felt about her well-girthed husband. Did being queen make up for having to be married to him?

I had expected to spend the evening listening to Pharaoh talk about how marvellous he was, but the more he drank, the quieter he grew. In fact, he seemed quite morose. I stifled a yawn and tried to look alert. Should I try to make conversation? Both Pharaoh and Isis seemed perfectly content to sit in silence. Maybe it was better to follow their example. It was easier anyway.

I tried to pretend I was occupied in watching the other diners. At least if nobody expected me to make conversation, it left me free to worry about Half.

CHAPTER 38

At last, Isis got to her feet. Her maids rushed forward to help her. She looked at me and I waited for her to speak, but she did no more than incline her head slightly in my direction. Then she left, her maids quickly falling into step behind her.

Pharaoh roused himself not long after and stumbled off without farewelling me. I was hardly surprised. The guard who had stood behind him all evening followed, and other guards who had been positioned around the hall filed out after them.

Did that mean I should leave? Did Ahmose's potion not work? I waited, wondering whether someone would tell me what to do, but felt increasingly awkward sitting alone on the dais, elevated above the other diners. I badly wanted to get back to the Palace of the Ornaments. Was Half still alive? Had Tall managed to find a way to tell someone what had happened? At last, I decided I could wait no longer. As I got to my feet, a guard came to escort me from the hall. We reached the door and he indicated for me to follow him.

"This way, my lady," he said.

"Isn't the entrance back that way?"

"It is. Pharaoh has asked that I show you to a chamber."

"For what purpose?"

The guard cleared his throat. "I couldn't say, my lady. It is not my place to ask such a question."

He led me to a comfortably appointed chamber that held a large bed and a number of couches. The guard cleared his throat again.

"My lady, you are to remove your gown and wait on the bed," he said. His gaze was fixed straight ahead, studiously avoiding my shocked face.

"Excuse me?"

"Those are Pharaoh's instructions."

"You can't be serious."

"My lady, I can only suggest you do as he says. It will go easier for you if you do."

He hurried out and closed the door softly behind him.

For a few moments, I considered fleeing. Had the guard gone, or did he wait in the hallway? It seemed unlikely the chamber would be left unguarded if Pharaoh was expected to be here shortly. Maybe I could run past the guard. Or I could feign illness and beg him to let me leave. I got as far as setting my hand to the knob, before I stopped.

This was why Father had sent me here. I was supposed to bear Pharaoh sons. I had spent my childhood being told that Father and Father alone would determine my future. That my sole reason for existing was to obey his will. This was what he wanted from me.

With trembling hands, I removed my gown and draped it over a couch. I smoothed the fabric and tried to pretend I wasn't waiting, naked, for the arrival of a man I barely knew. Please Marduk, don't let him do to me what he did to Ishtar.

I perched on the edge of the bed. Was I supposed to lie down? On top of the blanket or under it? Before I could decide, the door opened and two guards entered. Neither of them were the guard who had brought me here. They paid no attention to me sitting naked on the bed, blushing furiously, as they inspected the chamber. I assumed they were checking nobody hid in wait for Pharaoh. At last they left and he entered. I lay down. *Show Pharaoh what the women of Babylon are made of.*

Pharaoh never looked at me as he crossed the chamber and dropped his *shendyt* to the floor. He never said a word as he lay on top of me. I closed my eyes and tried to pretend it wasn't happening. Maybe I should have taken up Ahmose's offer of something to make it more pleasant.

Eventually, Pharaoh groaned and rolled off me. He rose from the bed, pulled on his *shendyt*, and left. He never once looked at me and he never spoke. I waited until the door closed before I got up. I tried to dress quickly, before any more guards came in, but my hands shook, the fabric tangled and twisted, and I couldn't get the gown on.

I tried again, more slowly this time. At last, my body was covered and I breathed a little easier. I straightened my wig and wished someone had thought to leave a hand mirror in here. When I opened the door, the guard who had brought me was waiting. He looked straight ahead as he spoke.

"Shall I show you to your transport, my lady?" he asked.

"Yes."

We said nothing else as he led me through the palace and out to where the slaves waited with the palanquin. Were these the same men who had carried me here, or had they gone, replaced by others? It hardly mattered.

The guard helped me to my seat and it was only then that his gaze darted to my face ever so quickly.

"Do you need anything else, my lady?" he asked.

His voice was more sympathetic than I expected, considering he had been trying hard not to look at me. Tears welled and I ducked my head before he could see.

"No," I said. "I'd like to leave now."

He stepped back and gestured towards the slave master. At their master's shout, the slaves raised the palanquin and we set off through the dark streets of Thebes.

My tears fell then and I didn't even try to stop them. Nobody would hear me crying above the sound of the slaves marching. Had Ahmose's potion worked? Was I already with child? Please, Marduk, let it be so. Let me not have to endure that again.

I cried all the way back to the Palace of the Ornaments. As we reached the gates, I wiped my face on the hem of my gown. My kohl was probably hopelessly smeared all over my face. There was no way to hide that I had been crying. All I could do was hold my head high and hope nobody commented.

The palanquin came to rest on the ground and a guard stepped forward to offer me his hand. The gates already stood open and I could feel the curious stares of the guards who waited there. I slipped inside and the gates closed behind me.

My tears started again. I covered my face with my hands as I sobbed.

"My lady."

Khaemmalu's voice was gentle as he took my elbow and moved me along the path. I let him lead me, painfully aware of how loud my sniffles were as I tried to get my tears under control. I desperately wanted to ask about Half, but I didn't think I could speak yet. Khaemmalu took me back to the sheltered spot, and by the time we got there, my sobs had mostly stopped, replaced with an occasional hiccup.

"Half?" I asked finally, not trusting my voice to manage anything else.

"He lives, for now. As far as I know, they made it to your chambers."

I could feel the questions he wanted to ask. If he had truly helped them, and hadn't revealed them to anyone, then he had proved himself to be an ally. I owed him an explanation, but I wanted to see Tall and Half safe with my own eyes first.

"Did you find out what happened?" I asked.

"Nothing more than we knew before you left. Ettu said Tall speaks of danger and a palace, but it's not clear whether he means here or Pharaoh's palace. We haven't been able to establish whether the attack was random or deliberate."

"Why would they target Half?" I asked. "He is of no threat to anyone."

"Perhaps he was in the wrong place at the wrong time. He may have seen or heard something he shouldn't have."

Half might have been searching for information that would be useful for me. Perhaps he had even uncovered something about Nebtu's disappearance.

Please Marduk, let him live. Not just for his own sake. Not just because he is a good man and he has done nothing wrong, but also so he can tell me what he discovered.

"My lady?"

I had almost forgotten Khaemmalu until he spoke again.

"Thank you," I said. "I don't have the words to express how

much I appreciate what you have done for me tonight. What you have done for all of us."

There would be time enough later to find out how they got Tall and Half to my chambers.

"Do you need anything else?" he asked.

"No. I just need to see him."

He nodded and took a step or two back.

"I shall leave you to go on from here alone then," he said. "We did what we could to make sure they weren't seen, but there is the risk that someone found them. We cannot be seen together."

"Yes, of course."

I stared at him for a moment, not knowing what else to say.

Khaemmalu gave me a short bow and disappeared into the shadows before I could say anything else.

As I hurried the rest of the way to the Palace, my mind was calmer than I might have expected. Nothing would be the same again after tonight. We had crossed a line, all of us, and we had involved an outsider. All my senses were telling me we could trust Khaemmalu, but I wouldn't have willingly involved him. Not in this. Not in smuggling two men — unmodified men — into my chambers. I couldn't imagine we would face anything less than execution if we were discovered.

How we would keep such a secret, I couldn't imagine, but for now the only thing we needed to worry about was ensuring Half lived. There would be time afterwards to plan. To decide whether we tried to keep them here in secret or if we should smuggle them out again.

If Half survived, perhaps I should send him and Tall away. Give them some of the jewels Father sent with me and tell them to make a new life for themselves, somewhere far away. Ettu would probably want to go with them and the knowledge that I would lose her made my heart hurt. She might think of me as nothing more than her mistress, but I had come to rely on her steady and practical guidance.

I saw nobody as I made my way up the three flights of stairs to my chambers. At least I would still have Ahmose and Merytre if Ettu left, and maybe I would invite another of my maids to move into my chambers. Sehener was a possibility. At the picnic, she was the one who seemed most willing to speak honestly to me.

As for me, I could only pray Pharaoh had managed to get me with child tonight. That was my purpose. What Father sent me here for. Bearing a son for Pharaoh mightn't be what I had ever envisioned for myself, but it was what my king required of me. All I had ever expected of my future was to do what my king wanted me to.

For the first time in my life, I wondered whether that would be enough for me.

* * *

Kassaya's journey continues in
Book 3: *Child of the Alliance*

ALSO BY KYLIE QUILLINAN

Palace of the Ornaments Series

Book One: *Princess of Babylon*

Book Two: *Ornament of Pharaoh*

Book Three: *Child of the Alliance*

Book Four: *A Game of Senet*

Book Five: *Secrets of Pharaoh*

Book Six: *Hawk of the West*

The Amarna Age Series

Book One: *Queen of Egypt*

Book Two: *Son of the Hittites*

Book Three: *Eye of Horus*

Book Four: *Gates of Anubis*

Book Five: *Lady of the Two Lands*

Book Six: *Guardian of the Underworld*

The Amarna Princesses Series

Book One: *Outcast*

Book Two: *Catalyst*

Book Three: *Warrior*

See kyliequillinan.com for more books, including exclusive collections, and newsletter sign up.

ABOUT THE AUTHOR

Kylie writes about women who defy society's expectations. Her novels are for readers who like fantasy with a basis in history or mythology. Her interests include Dr Who, jellyfish and cocktails. She needs to get fit before the zombies come.

Swan – the epilogue to the Tales of Silver Downs series – is available exclusively to her newsletter subscribers. Sign up at kyliequillinan.com.